"Do you have any idea of the risk you took?

"Of the risk you put your team in?" Stone, her instructor, continued, his voice a wall of icy rage.

"Are you angry because we completed the mission or because we didn't fail?" Vaughn shot back.

It was inevitable that he wouldn't have approved of her means to accomplish her mission, if for no other reason than she was team leader, and he wasn't exactly her biggest fan.

But she wasn't going to let him win at this point. She'd taken a major step along the path to her dream. Hers and hers alone. Not her father's, not her mother's, not her society peers'.

Stone was wrong. Her parents were wrong. She did have something to give, to offer. She'd lived in that other world already—glitzy, glamorous nothingness—and she wasn't going back. She was here and she was going to stay.

Dear Reader,

The concept for *Invisible Recruit* came from a TV documentary about the ninja of feudal Japan. Different than the traditional warrior class of samurai, the ninja became legendary for their powers to blend into the shadows and disappear. In truth, ninja often hid in plain sight, assuming their roles of shopkeepers, tradesmen and farmers. When hunted by those who wished to harm them, these "invisible" people blended in so well with the civilian population that no one was the wiser. Another little-known fact about ninja is that there were women ninja as well as men. It didn't take a large leap of imagination to conjure modern-day ninja women, without the unisex black outfits, who could go where their more official, and mostly male counterparts could not go, simply because no one looked beyond their ordinary-world occupations of society debutante, hairdresser, teacher and more.

I hope you enjoy seeing beneath these women's exterior occupations to their powerful interior lives as much as I've enjoyed learning about them.

Regards,

Mary Buckham

INVISIBLE
RECRUIT

Mary Buckham

BOMBSHELL™

Published by Silhouette Books

America's Publisher of Contemporary Romance

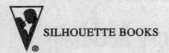 SILHOUETTE BOOKS

ISBN 0-373-51406-9

INVISIBLE RECRUIT

Copyright © 2006 by Mary E. Buckham

All rights reserved. Except for use in any review, the reproduction or utilization of this work in whole or in part in any form by any electronic, mechanical or other means, now known or hereafter invented, including xerography, photocopying and recording, or in any information storage or retrieval system, is forbidden without the written permission of the editorial office, Silhouette Books, 233 Broadway, New York, NY 10279 U.S.A.

All characters in this book have no existence outside the imagination of the author and have no relation whatsoever to anyone bearing the same name or names. They are not even distantly inspired by any individual known or unknown to the author, and all incidents are pure invention.

This edition published by arrangement with Harlequin Books S.A.

® and TM are trademarks of Harlequin Books S.A., used under license. Trademarks indicated with ® are registered in the United States Patent and Trademark Office, the Canadian Trade Marks Office and in other countries.

www.SilhouetteBombshell.com

Printed in U.S.A.

Books by Mary Buckham

Silhouette Bombshell

Invisible Recruit #92

Intimate Moments

The Makeover Mission #1308

*IR-5

MARY BUCKHAM

has always believed in make-believe. As a child she roped, cajoled and bullied her brothers and sisters, along with any unsuspecting neighbor child, into elaborate story productions put on in her backyard or basement. Roles included swashbuckling pirates, damsels in distress, and heroes and heroines—this was Mary's role—who saved the day. As an adult, Mary made sure her five children had a trunk of dress-up clothes and plenty of space to create their own make-believe worlds. She married her Prince Charming, one who doesn't mind that she talks with imaginary people and who learned to cook as a self-preservation measure. She lives in a picturesque Pacific Northwest seaport community filled with writers, artists and musicians, all constantly proving that the power of make-believe can make magic happen. Mary loves hearing from readers, writers and everyone in between. You can reach her via her Web site, www.marybuckham.com.

Chapter 1

Vaughn Monroe hesitated, unsure for a second, hugging the brick wall and peering into the darkness beyond. The smell of spring dampened the night air. A whip-poor-will's trill was cut off midnote with crickets playing beyond the mowed grass. Traffic far down the valley hummed past while her heart beat shallow and fast.

Had she killed him? Or should she have tried harder?

The run uphill had been rough, guided only by the moon glowing overhead and the vapor arc lamp in the opening between buildings that hunkered down in the stillness, obsidian slabs casting more shadows.

She'd trained for this, anticipated the drill inside and out. But knowing and doing were worlds apart. How many had he said? Five total? She'd counted four down. One to go.

Not bad for a deb. *Take that, Stone, and stuff it up your backside.*

She crouched lower, not wasting much effort on celebrating. Yet. Not while he could still be out there. Somewhere. Waiting.

Overextended muscles cramped in her lower stomach, mimicking those in clenched fingers cradling the modified Walther PPK. She ignored everything except the space before her. She hadn't come here to fail. This time she was going to win. Two hundred yards and she was home free. Another quick scan as she swallowed hard.

She should have made sure she'd taken him out back at the creek. Maybe it'd been enough. But the man was like Lazarus—killing him meant nothing.

She stepped forward, heard the brush of her crepe-soled boots against the gravel.

Damn!

She froze, breath stalling in her lungs, muscles quaking, sweat trickling along her lower back.

He was there. She knew it.

Waiting. Watching. Anticipating.

He wanted to stop her.

Tough. Let him want.

Nothing.

When pinpricks circled her vision she gave in, gulping a ragged fistful of cool air. Only then did she move forward into the shadows.

Wall to her left, steel building to the right. Objective at four o'clock.

Where would she hide if she were him?

Straight in front of her. Downwind. Easier to hear movement. He'd stay south of the objective, where the darkness deepened between two buildings.

She smiled, stood and crept forward. Ten feet. Eight. *Almost there. Stay focused, no time to get cocky.*

Five.

A whisper of cloth against cloth. That was all.

Too late.

She whirled. The slam of a shoulder careened along her rib cage, twisting her, rolling, her back punched against packed gravel. She couldn't inhale, couldn't move.

A knee slammed to her chest. Hand to her throat. Pressing.

He had her. And there wasn't a damn thing she could do about it.

"You're dead," he whispered, leaning so close his breath warmed her face. "Mission failed."

Lights blazed on all around them. The exercise was finished. She swallowed the defeat clogging her throat, telling herself it was physical pain but knowing she was lying.

She noted only his eyes, inches from hers.

Death promised less pain than they did.

This wasn't over. Not by a long shot.

Vaughn leaned against the steel curve of the Quonset hut, aware of every movement around her. The other agents in training were as tired, as ragged as she was. Two weeks ago, they had been only names; now they were her team. Not yet friends, if ever. They'd all come here with an agenda, a job to do, and friendship wasn't it. But here and now, she accepted their thoughts as her own, their disappointment mirroring hers, their aches and bruises shadowing her own. Almost.

The thrum of pain beating across her ribs sang a familiar dirge. Stone had scored this time. It wasn't the first, but one of these days, soon, she'd make sure it was the last.

"The man isn't human," Alexis "Alex" Noziak muttered at her side, collapsed over her gear pack, her straight blue-black Native American hair hiding the frustration in her expression but not in her voice. "Maybe he's one of those demon creatures who work at night to feast on mere mortals. He even looks like he could be the devil's spawn. Dark hair, dark eyes, body to die for, but even that could be just temptation working for him."

"So how do you explain that he's as hard-edged during the day as he is at night?" Kelly McAlister asked in her soft Kansas accent.

"Can't." Alex sighed, leaning her head back and twisting her neck like a rag doll. "My momma told me never to trust dark-eyed men who are too good-looking for their own good."

Vaughn scraped together enough energy for a smile. Alex told it as she saw it. Nothing hidden in this Idaho girl. But would that trait backfire as their training continued? One more excuse for Stone to cull their already dwindling numbers. Week two, and they'd lost four recruits so far. After tonight there'd most likely be more. Who'd have thought volunteers could be thinned like debs at their first outing. Systematically picked off until none were left. Even the government had to accept and keep some of its new hires, but not Stone. If he continued as he'd begun, the Agency would end before it began.

Not her problem. Her problem was to make sure if any probies were left, she'd be one of them. Damn and double damn. She should have—

Failure clogged her throat.

She shrugged against the cold metal seeping through her fatigues. Too bad it did nothing to chill the churning in her gut.

"Attention," Jayleen called to her right. Jayleen was the most stunningly beautiful black woman Vaughn had ever met. All angles, large obsidian eyes and attitude armor-thick around her. An attitude Vaughn had yet to get through.

She heard bodies shifting, no doubt in response to Jayleen's command. As if all eyes weren't already riveted on the man entering the empty building. He walked like he taught—arrogant, assured and always in control. Alex was right. The man wasn't human. He was a robo-instructor sent to make life a misery for all of them. And he did a fine job of it.

M. T. Stone.

No one knew what the initials stood for. On the first day, they'd guessed Mighty Tough; by the third day, it'd become Mostly Terminal. The polite terms had disappeared by the end of the first week.

A few recruits shifted. One, in addition to Jayleen, stood. The rest remained where they were, like Vaughn, not sure if their legs would hold them.

"Anyone want to explain why no one made the objective tonight?" He strode forward, boots silent against the concrete floor, his voice as dark as he was, his gaze lethal as it swept over the two dozen women huddled on one side. Vaughn didn't need to glance at her watch to know sunrise was less than an hour away; exhaustion gave the time away. They'd been at this exercise for more than twenty hours. And it looked as if it wouldn't be over for a while.

"Poor execution, sir." Jayleen stepped forward like the butt-kisser she was.

Eyes as hard as the man's name slid toward the former con artist. She called herself a tarot card reader, but the rumor about this recruit's background already raced like wildfire among them. Jayleen stood a heartbeat from jail time unless she got her act together, regardless of whether she looked like a cover model. Everyone had their own reason for joining IR5, their own motivation for facing hell, and Stone, on a daily basis. Too bad Vaughn couldn't call upon it.

Stone continued, his voice cutting through the group, his gaze still pinning Jayleen. "Poor execution? Is that what the problem was?"

Vaughn actually felt sorry for the woman. *Duck, Jayleen, the man's hunting for heads.*

He shifted, zeroing in on Vaughn as if beading a rifle scope. He wanted blood. That wasn't news. He'd settle for hers. But that wasn't news, either.

"Do you agree, *deb?* Poor execution?"

"No." She didn't bother to shift more than her gaze until it locked with his. She'd make him work for every ounce of blood he drew from her. Blood, sweat and tears. Churchill had it right. The great statesman understood the price of survival, but he forgot the cost of pride.

"So you think you executed tonight's exercise well?" Stone's tone taunted.

"No."

"Can't have it both ways, princess. Which is it?"

"We screwed up. We gave it our best, but it wasn't good enough."

"If that's your best, you'd all be dead."

Man had a point. And he knew she knew it. "Agreed."

"You think that's going to get you off the hook?"

Not with this man.

"No."

Something hot and dangerous came and went in his eyes.

"You've finally gotten something right, Monroe."

Calling her *deb* or *princess* was bad enough, but when he used her last name, the crap was about to hit the fan. She refused to move, keeping her hands flat and open at her sides even as the muscles in her stomach locked into a granite block. He would not break her. She would not let him.

She said nothing.

His eyes goaded, daring her to fight back.

Suicide.

"Sir?" Alex's voice slashed the tension. "We almost—"

"There is no almost in this business." Stone didn't even bother to look at Alex. Instead he stepped closer to Vaughn, towering over where she sat, using size as a weapon. Not that he needed one with that malt-whiskey-over-ice voice. It could kill all on its own. "No second chances. No do-overs. Monroe should have taken me out when she had the chance. She didn't. Three shots on target. None lethal. She should have confirmed—it's the way of a true operative."

Truth wasn't always painless.

"Stand." The word commanded, even when spoken so low that most recruits couldn't hear it.

She used the steel at her back to give her courage as she rose to her feet, locking her legs into a stance as rigid as the man before her.

Her gaze shifted upward to meet his.

And to think she'd actually volunteered for this. Next time she wanted to prove something, to herself or to her family, she'd take up bungee jumping. Unfortunately, she already had. And skydiving, and—finding one's niche was hell some days.

"Nothing to say for yourself, deb?"

She glanced at the neon yellow paint stain dampening his right shoulder. He was right. She'd taken her shots. Knew even then they might not be lethal. And moved on. Too scared to find out if she'd failed. Not trusting that she might have won.

"No." She was glad her voice didn't quiver.

"You screwed up."

Yup, sure did. She remained mute.

"You do that in the field and you kill your team members. Understand?"

It was a low blow. And effective.

"Yes." The word congealed chalklike along her throat.

"You kill yourself, no loss. You kill them and the mission fails. Unacceptable."

Those were not tears acid-etching her eyes. She wouldn't let them be. She wouldn't give him the pleasure of knowing he could get to her.

He leaned closer, his words sandpapering across her. "Do you understand?"

Her hands curled without thought. She watched his gaze shift to them, aware that he'd scored. Again.

"Understand?" he repeated, this time his voice lower and huskier. An intimate sound. Between the two of them. Promise and warning.

"Yes."

"If you can't kill, you don't belong here."

His eyes said what his words didn't. *You don't belong here anyway.* It was an old refrain, communicated in a hundred ways over the last two weeks. He wanted her off the team and out of the Agency. No former ambassador's daughters allowed. No room for debutantes, for a fast-living, high-society woman seeking a new thrill. His words, his phrases again and again, echoing her own fears.

Holding his gaze, no matter what the price, she

offered her mother-trained smile, knowing it'd only make the next months even more unbearable. As if that were possible.

"I won't make that mistake again." She spoke to him and him alone. "Next time I kill you, I'll make sure you're dead."

For a heartbeat, she thought he'd smile, but that would make him human. And this man didn't do human.

Instead he said nothing, stepped back, pivoted and strode to the center of the room.

"Again."

No one dared moan. A few closed their eyes. Vaughn remained still.

"Twenty seconds. Lower field."

Then he was gone.

"The man's a sadist," Alex said, voicing their collective thoughts.

"He knows what he's doing." It was Jayleen speaking, earning the previously suppressed groans. She ignored the group and turned toward Vaughn. "He's right and you know it. You had the chance to end the exercise and didn't take it."

"There was another op out there," Kelly interjected, playing peacemaker, something she no doubt had learned on the playground of the private school where she taught kindergarten. A hard role to play when you were the size of a Barbie doll facing a tank in a woman's body.

Jayleen glanced at the other, sensing an easier mark to attack, but Vaughn deflected her.

"Jayleen's right. Stone's right. I screwed up."

Jayleen's eyes widened, letting her surprise show, something Stone would never do. "So because of you we all have to go through this again."

"That's right, darling." Vaughn didn't wait for Jayleen's retort. She was small potatoes compared to Stone, who was even now waiting for them at the lower field, no doubt counting the seconds until he put them through their grueling paces and waiting for her to screw up. Again.

Too bad. This time he wouldn't be the one winning. This time, she was.

Stone a sadist? Possibly. Good at what he did? Oh, yeah. Nemesis? No doubt. But none of it mattered. He thought he had her number, but he was wrong, and she was about to prove it.

"Come on, ladies," she said to those closest, then smiled through the pain as she pushed herself off the wall. "Let's kill the bastard this time."

Ling Mai strolled to where M.T. leaned, arms braced on the metal rail encircling the balcony overlooking the sparring ground. A dozen women dressed in *gis* paired off below them, the white martial-arts outfits stark against red mats. Traditional dojo shouts of *"Kai"* and *"Keyah"* rang in the afternoon air.

He looked tired. Not that anyone else could tell. But she'd known her new lead instructor long enough to read the nuances beneath his stoic exterior, an asset in his profession but which took its toll on him as a human being.

"I understand you ran two full ops last night." She stopped beside him, keeping her stance casual.

He didn't glance her way. "They screwed up first round."

"Heard you were hit, though. That's a first."

His jaw slid back and forth. "Hit but not taken out. Monroe has the instincts of a gnat. She won't survive long in this business."

Interesting. He'd mentioned this particular recruit by name more than once already. Ling Mai glanced at her hands, folded one on top of the other on the steel railing. "And yet she got close enough to take a hit on you. More than one, from what I hear. Surely that shows promise?"

He glanced at her. Not an easy look, but then he wasn't an easy man. "She's a debutante, not an operative. She's a thrill junkie, using becoming an agent as she would any other new sport, new experience. It's a game to her, a temporary phase that'll dissipate the minute it's no longer fun. You and I both know she doesn't belong here."

"She has other assets." Ling Mai let her gaze drift to the woman they spoke about, knowing Stone's would follow. The brunette was holding her own, paired against the former—what did she call herself?—tarot reader, Jayleen Smart, even though Jayleen weighed a good fifteen pounds more. Both women were tall, dark-haired and in good shape, but the comparison ended there.

Jayleen was street trained and savvy, a graduate of the school of hard knocks. She'd learned at an early age there was no one but herself to depend upon in the jungle of life. She might look like the Queen of Sheba by the way she carried herself, but the only kingdom she'd ever ruled was a stretch of Chicago's lower South Side.

Vaughn looked like a ballet dancer compared to her, light and agile on her feet, using speed and dexterity against the other's more solid moves and lunges. Her polished looks belonged on glossy magazine pages; in real life, she had graced more than one cover.

Was that why she disturbed Stone? In their business, anonymity was a plus. An agent needed to blend into the locale, not stand out.

Stone was an exception to that rule, and it'd never hurt him. In their former assignments, his looks had been used time and again as a lure. So it seemed strange that he'd hold Vaughn's cover-model face and body against her. Did the fact that Vaughn looked like fine porcelain instead of sturdy stoneware make him want to shelter the woman from the harsh realities of their world? If so, that could raise a problem.

Ling Mai would keep an eye on the situation. She intended to use Vaughn for the Russian op as soon as the woman could hold her own. Stone would understand soon enough that Ling Mai had chosen well. In the meantime, he had a job to do and he'd do it. She hired only the best and was determined that this new program succeed. All she needed was the initial team, a group of strong, determined women—no less than five, no more than seven—who could prove that Ling Mai's theory would work.

Keeping her voice level, she asked, "And the others? You've already cut six."

"You're asking for the impossible here and you know it. They have no background for this, outside the odd sport here or there. I'll be lucky if I can keep any of them." He didn't bother to hide the frustration in his tone or in the pointed look he shot her.

"We've covered this before, M.T."

"And you know where I stand. You want cannon fodder, you ask someone else to do this."

"You're the best." Then she added the selling point. "You also know you're their only chance."

He exhaled, as telling as a shouted curse from any other man.

"And if they're not ready?" he asked, kneading his right shoulder and the scar branded there.

"You'll make them ready. There is no choice."

He turned back, bracing his hands against the hard metal railing, his gaze surveying the women below. Ling Mai noted where his glance immediately rested.

Very interesting.

She said nothing, waiting in silence for Stone's unasked question.

His voice sounded even wearier than earlier. "Is there any other way to reach your objective?"

"Meaning going back to trained law enforcement recruits instead of these women?"

"Exactly."

"I've told you before, this is an experiment." She shrugged, but it did little to ease the tension clutching her shoulders. A tension no one but she carried in this endeavor. "It might work, it might not, but we'll never know if we don't take the risk. The alphabet agencies have lost too many undercover operatives recently for us not to think outside the box."

"This isn't out of the box, this is off the damn screen."

"I agree that these women don't have the standard background of more traditional undercover agents, but I believe that's in their favor."

He nodded toward the women below. "You're talking about hairdressers and con artists here, Ling Mai. And a bloody kindergarten teacher."

"And one debutante."

His jaw tightened, another telling gesture from a man who rarely betrayed any.

After a moment's silence shimmered and cooled between them, he asked, "How big an operation is this?"

She'd been waiting for this question and regretted she could not offer him more at this time.

"In terms of assets?" she asked, buying a moment.

"In terms of importance. Any chance the team you're assembling could be mixed? Include a few seasoned ops with these newbies?"

She'd considered the option, and discarded it, knowing the direction she planned on taking the Agency, knowing, too, the team was intended for more than an immediate assignment. Their world was filled with impossible choices, and this was just another one of them.

"Unfortunately it might cause problems."

"Problems? Is there a leak?"

The man always went for the jugular.

"No. Not that we know of."

He pressed. "You don't trust me, Ling Mai?"

"Never crossed my mind." That was the truth. She trusted his skills, his loyalty and his discretion, the last a valuable commodity in their profession. "You shall find out all you need to know in due time."

He slanted her a crooked grin. It didn't soften his face. "As in several months of time?"

"Something like that."

"You are a very hard woman, Ling Mai."

"As you are a very hard man, M.T."

The grin slipped away. She regretted keeping him in the dark for even the short duration, but tucked the thought aside, looking once again at the women below.

"What about McAlister? The schoolteacher." Ling Mai focused their attention on the petite blonde looking as out of place on the dojo floor as Stone would in the woman's home turf, the cornfields of Kansas.

Stone gave a shrug. "Not bad. Not as bad as I expected."

"But?"

"Time will tell. She reminds me of my third-grade teacher. Marshmallow soft covering a core of steel."

"I still hear a *but*, M.T."

"I don't know if she'll ever be a field agent."

"She's done some community theater in her hometown. That should help. It's in her file."

"Playacting is not the same as undercover work and we both know it. Besides, all the files are scant when it comes down to real info. I'd say they were pretty well culled over before being passed along to me." His gaze slid to Vaughn again.

"The files were meant to give you enough to start with and let you form your own opinions."

"And if I buy that line, you have a swamp in Florida to sell me."

She gave him a real smile. "A very nice swamp, M.T."

His gaze shifted back to the blonde now pinned to the mat, giving her opponent an atta-girl grin. "McAlister will probably make it. If she stays away from Monroe."

"Problems between the two?"

"Not per se. McAlister has a savior complex. Might work behind a desk, or with five-year-olds, but could cause problems in the field."

"Are you saying McAlister steps in to save Monroe?"

"Like the country mouse saving the city cat. Not necessary. But McAlister tends to act as a deflective shield around the other and Monroe doesn't stop it enough."

"Does she need to?"

"Not yet. But it's a bad habit to develop. Debutante using the peasant as a shield."

"Pretty harsh."

"I'm not here to pretty up the picture."

He was right. Ling Mai glanced at another of the recruits. "And Alexis Noziak?"

"A bulldog. You could tell she was raised with brothers. You say she's a hairdresser?"

"The correct term is beautician. She does nails, too."

"I'll keep that in mind." He gave her a reluctant grin, before adding, "The surprise is that she's acting like McAlister around Monroe. Stepping in to show her how to drop, roll and run. Puts in extra time with her on the dojo floor."

"We *are* building a team here." She allowed a pleased hum to escape. Maybe her theory had promise after all.

"It'll be my team. The members I select to work together. Not a girls' club and certainly not Monroe's."

Was this the problem then? Was the tension humming between Vaughn and M.T. any time they were near each other a power struggle—one leading by instinct, the other creating a logical, cohesive whole? They didn't have to be mutually exclusive goals, as long as Stone could accept and respect an agent bred from a different type of woman. Accept and work side by side with an agent whose assets lay not in her law-enforcement background but in other skills and abilities. Ones invisible to most people.

Ling Mai decided not to push for answers. Yet. The answers would show themselves soon enough. "And what about Jayleen Smart? The tarot reader."

"Is that what we're calling her?"

"It will do."

He ignored the bait, and instead answered, "She's good. Very good. Probably stands the best chance of staying the duration."

How much did Jayleen's progress have to do with incentive? In some ways, she was their biggest risk. Her background made her different from the other women. So did Vaughn's, for that matter. Opposite ends of the spectrum.

Ling Mai glanced at the two women still sparring with each other, perspiration darkening their *gis* visible from here. She wondered if she should ask Stone to increase their training schedule. Less than three weeks before the Russian made his first move. But if Stone knew that, would he wash his hands of the whole project here and now? Choices, it always came down to choices.

"And Jayleen's interactions with Monroe?" Ling Mai kept her tone neutral. Monroe slapped Jayleen to the mat with a double backward twist, then held out her hand to help her opponent up. It was ignored.

"Water and oil." Stone shook his head. "No love lost between those two."

"Any obvious reason why?"

"No clue."

Stone was the type who made sure he understood his students inside and out before he'd allow them to pass training, even if the staff psychologist cleared them. If there were something going on between two potential agents, he'd know why. Probably already did. But he wasn't saying.

In this she'd trust him. For now. She had her own theories as to what was happening and would explore them more closely. She would hold her questions.

She turned toward Stone. "Will you have Monroe stop by my office when she is free?"

Stone's look asked questions, but he only nodded.

"Then I shall leave you to your work." She turned on her stiletto heels to leave.

"Ling Mai?" He straightened away from the rail, his gaze brooding.

"Yes?"

"If she isn't ready I *will* eliminate her from the team, regardless of whether she's one of your handpicked ones."

There was no need to say who *she* was.

"You forget, M.T. They are all my handpicked ones." Each and every one with a skill that no training could enhance and that would serve its purpose in due time.

"It's not like you to sidestep the hard issues."

"As it is not like you to question my judgment." She let an edge coat her tone.

"It's not your judgment I'm questioning. I've never approved of slaughter."

Neither did she. Which was why she had chosen Stone to lead and train them. She hadn't lied earlier when she had acknowledged he was their best hope. He might be their only hope. "Your concerns are duly noted."

"Noted and discarded."

"You are looking at only a portion of the picture," she reminded him gently, her need for discretion not his fault. "I am looking at a larger image."

He took the rebuke silently, as she'd known he would.

She walked away, knowing the issue was unresolved. An unusual occurrence. He hated to lose an operative, whereas she knew that sometimes there was no choice.

Chapter 2

Vaughn faced Alex on the dojo floor, bouncing lightly on the balls of her feet. Alex would give her best, but Vaughn was confident she could hold her own. After trouncing Jayleen, anything was possible.

"You've improved." Alex wiped sweat from her forehead. "Last week I could take you no problem."

"That was last week," Vaughn said with a grin.

"Want to put a twenty on the fact that your luck's about to change?"

Vaughn laughed out loud. "Luck has nothing to do with it. Double it and it's a bet."

"You're on."

Vaughn stepped back, only to run into a wall of muscle. She froze.

"If you ladies have time for jokes here, then you must not be working hard enough."

Alex straightened and Vaughn did the same. Stone crossed from behind her to stand between them, his expression as unforgiving as his words.

"It wasn't that, sir," Alex started before Vaughn's look stuttered her into silence.

What was the point? If the other woman explained the difference between a joke and competition, Stone would just go harder on her. Vaughn was the target here, not Alex.

Stone must have noted the exchanged look, or had been expecting it. He turned toward Vaughn and she caught herself working not to stiffen.

"So, deb, you want to explain the joke? Share it with the group."

"There was no joke."

"Are you saying I didn't hear you two laughing?"

"I was unaware sparring was to be done like machines, sir. Without emotion." At one time, Vaughn had understood the concept of discretion. Not that she'd ever been very good about implementing it.

Alex sucked in her breath as Stone stepped closer to Vaughn, those black, black eyes of his narrowing.

He towered above her. "Emotions can get you killed in the field."

"I'll embroider that on a pillow."

There *was* a snicker somewhere behind her. The whole group would pay for her inability to hold her tongue. But she'd pay first.

Fine. Bring it on.

"You think this is a joke, Monroe?"

"No."

"Out of the way, Noziak." He barked the order to Alex as he stepped face-to-face with Vaughn, his movement automatically slipping into a warrior's stance. "We'll see how the debutante feels about emotion after she faces a real fight."

At last. Just the two of them, going at it.

Vaughn's vision narrowed, focusing only on Stone, accentuating every sharp angle of his face, the determination darkening his eyes. Adrenaline surged through her, giving her a heady sensation. Or maybe it was fear. Around this man, they were twins.

She stepped back, circling as he was, blocking out the others moving in closer for the show. A universal response to bloodletting.

Stone was larger, stronger and way more experienced than she. But she had something he didn't. A reason to fight. For him, this was a lesson; for her, it was payback. She might go down in agony, most likely would, but she'd get a few licks in first. And those dangerous eyes of his, if nothing else, told her he understood where she was coming from.

He made the first move. A half feint forward, one a child could have dodged.

Watch his eyes. Not his body. Watch them telegraph his next move. Wasn't that what he'd been drilling into them for weeks?

Except he forgot to tell them robo-instructors didn't telegraph anything.

His next move came hard and fast, his shoulder to hers as his foot swept hers out from under her. She was on her back and beneath him between the space of one heartbeat and another. Her breath siphoned from her lungs, freezing her for a pulse beat too long.

He leaned over her, elbow to collarbone, knee pinning her pelvis.

"Ready to quit, deb?"

Dream on, big guy. Not in this lifetime.

She dropped her gaze, glancing to the right. The pressure along her throat lessened.

His first mistake. She swallowed her grin before it reached her lips.

Her curled fists shot out, slamming into his muscled sides, catching his kidneys.

She didn't wait but rolled to the left. Twice. Her feet were still tangled with his legs, but she could breathe again.

He lunged after her.

One knee up deflected him.

Get off the floor. Don't let him use his weight and strength against you.

One steel hand grabbed her calf, tugging her toward him. She countered with her heel, catching him center stomach.

She used his body as a fulcrum, pushing back as he doubled forward. Seconds only, but it allowed her to break free.

She clambered to her feet, never turning her back on him. He came to his knees, his gaze razor sharp.

Her breath chugged in and out while he looked as if he hadn't broken a sweat. The bastard. How could she beat the unbeatable? Maybe she couldn't, but that didn't mean she wouldn't try. As long as there was breath left in her body, she'd give it her best shot. She hadn't come here to fail, and not at the hands of Mighty Tough Stone.

She anchored her feet on the mat. A voice let out a *hurrah* in the circle tightening around them both.

She ignored it.

He stood. Slowly. Calmly. Deliberately.

They mirrored each other's moves. Two pendulums swaying opposite one another, both wary, both looking for the slightest of opportunities.

He wouldn't make the same mistake again. Ball in her court. Time for her to play the game using her own rules.

She moved fast, using speed against his size. Her head slammed into his gut, a solid thud against a rock wall.

It mimicked the story of her life. Always running head-on into someone's opposition—her father's, her mother's, her position in society. All telling her loud and clear to give up, stop fighting the inevitable, go with the flow. Telling her they knew what was best for her. Telling her, as Stone had told her since the first day of training, to walk away. Be less than she could be. Be what they defined her as, not how she defined herself. She was not a society interloper, a debutante whose only purpose was decorative, and useless. She was

Vaughn, and Stone was about to find out what that meant.

His hands clamped around her arms, pinning them at the waist, lifting in the same move.

She let him pull forward, leveraging her feet with a push off from the floor, sinking her head. A backward pivot she learned from a French gymnast.

Her feet sprang up, locking around his neck. She'd be lucky if she didn't break her own.

A hard tuck and he was off balance, falling forward. He twisted, letting go of her to save them both.

She'd counted on it. Spiraling as she hit the floor, almost beneath him, but not quite, just enough to execute a quick squirm, backflip, palms to floor, and she was on her feet.

A round of applause erupted.

"You go, girl!" Alex shouted.

"They're going to kill each other."

"My money's on Stone." Jayleen's tone sounded final, and very cocky.

Vaughn blocked out the voices, her attention focused on the man rising to his knees. He was her nemesis. He wanted her cowed and whipped and beaten, and she wasn't going to give him the satisfaction.

"Nice move, Monroe. Didn't learn that here."

"Gymnastics class. Eight years."

He actually grinned. It caught her off guard, stalled her response by seconds. Big mistake around him.

He was up and attacking before she could move more than a step back. But it was all she needed. A fast hop, right leg up, double pirouette, and her ankle caught him in the throat.

Another would have crashed. He gasped. The hit had to hurt like Hades. She still remembered the time she had used it against Juillet Fouquet in seventh grade. Payback for a school year of bullying an underclassman.

He pulled back.

"And that?" he asked, his voice slightly huskier than before. Point to her—she'd made him sweat, which outlined the flatness of his abs. Point to him that she'd noticed.

"Ballet."

"I'll remember that."

Then he moved, faster than she could inhale.

A blur rushed at her. A wave of muscle crashed against her.

She went down. Hard. All breath soundlessly leeched from her body, lights tap-dancing across her vision.

"And this, princess, is called street fighting."

Another embroidered pillow, she thought, even as her vision grayed.

"Give up?" The sound of his dark-chocolate voice washed against her, then receded. A caress with a slice.

Hands bit into her arms. "Don't you dare—"

Dare what?

Pressure eased. Black shifted to gray, then lightened as air slowly seeped back into her lungs. She might live after all; she wasn't sure if that was good news or bad.

"Lesson over, class." Bare feet swished against mats, shuffling away, murmured voices receding.

He was standing now. When had he moved?

She rolled, every muscle screaming in agony, buying a few seconds to keep from puking on the dojo floor.

"Get up, Monroe."

Why? So he could kill her face-to-face? Or expel her?

The last thought gave her motion. No way would she let him kick her out of the program while she lolled on the floor like a loser.

She shifted from side to knees, then stood. The quake of her muscles made it doubtful that she could hold the position for long. By propping her hands against her knees, though, she could do it. The only thing keeping her upright was the sound of Stone's deeper breathing. He'd won, but she'd made him work at it.

She expected him to crow, but leave it to the man to simply stand there until she raised her gaze to his, catching a question in his eyes before they shifted.

"Ling Mai wants to see you."

"Ling Mai?" It came on a pant of breath.

"Her office. Main building."

This was it, then. Expulsion. The bastard had gotten his way.

"Not yet, princess," he said, as if reading her thoughts. "Soon, but not yet."

He strolled away.

It was a ploy her parents had used. Slash and cut from their moral high ground, then walk away. There could be no fight if there was no opponent.

She pulled herself upright, caught Alex's and Kelly's concerned glances from across the room and gave them a shaky nod. No one would know the price of the last few moments. But they were worth it. Maybe M.T. meant Mighty Tempting to knock that superiority off his face.

She actually found herself grinning, along with a few winces as she wobbled toward the showers. There was another battle to face. Another chance to cut and run, as Stone wanted, or hold her ground, shaky though it might be. A call to the director's office was not to be ignored.

Vaughn glanced around the elegantly appointed room, not surprised to see the juxtaposition of Eastern and Western tastes. The Sung dynasty blue-and-white pottery gracing the top of a Louis XIV gilt-edged table, a Thai silk weaving thrown casually across a leather chair.

She had sat in many such rooms over the years while her father took up his various government posts and her mother followed, two daughters in tow. One resenting each move, fighting the upheaval and change, burying the inevitable behind a facade of anger, morphing into bad-girl action. In Paris, Vienna, D.C. and Kuala Lumpur.

"I hope I have not kept you waiting." Ling Mai glided into the room with her graceful walk. They'd known each other at least ten years, though their family ties went back further. But Ling Mai was not a woman who let others into her private thoughts, not even old family friends.

Vaughn stood, wincing slightly at the ache of muscles and fresh bruises. "Not at all, it's been nice to have a break." Then she cursed her slip of the tongue, not wanting the other woman to think she was complaining or telling tales out of turn.

"Please sit. You look tired."

Since Ling Mai was quite aware of the training happening in other areas of the large Maryland estate, there was no need for polite prevarication.

"I am tired. Though it feels good in its own warped way." She allowed a smile to lighten her words, priding herself on her ability to see the irony in life. "A little hard work never hurt anyone."

"Would you like tea?" Ling Mai made it more statement than question. "I believe Earl Grey is your preference."

Vaughn swallowed her surprise. There was little unknown to Ling Mai. The ageless woman no doubt knew every detail of her recruits' past lives and current preferences. That made for a formidable hostess, and agent, a role Ling Mai played with the best.

"That sounds heavenly."

The other woman smiled and punched an intercom on her otherwise clear desk. "Dewhurst. Hot tea, please. Earl Grey and Lapsang souchong."

A pleasant silence hung between the two, backed by the sound of water sliding gently down a stone fountain in a corner of the room. Meant to soothe and refresh. Again, typical of countless drawing rooms and casual social functions Vaughn had attended.

There'd be pleasantries exchanged, small talk made until refreshments were served, nothing of note undertaken until polite rituals were observed. How comfortable and reassuring it all was, especially after the last weeks where it seemed Vaughn could do no right. Two women, sitting quietly in a well-appointed room.

"Your parents are well?" Ling Mai sat back in her brocaded chair, her fingers steepled together beneath her chin.

"As far as I know."

"They are unaware you are here?"

"I felt it best." Vaughn wondered at the tap dance. The ramifications if her parents, especially her father, became aware of this undertaking, were far-reaching. Not that he'd stay in the dark for long. The man's career required intimate and immediate knowledge of such situations. "No fallout for the Agency, I can assure you. As for explaining what I am doing here—" she ignored the tenseness in her shoulders "—there will be time to talk to them. Later."

If she passed. If she didn't, it was a moot point; they would never need to know. A dream dying silently, one that never would meet with their approval anyway. An image of Stone rose before her.

"Yes. It is wise." Ling Mai's voice sounded as lyrical and soothing as if they were discussing the change of seasons. "And your sister? Chrissie?"

Sore point, best to quickly gloss over. "The children and her husband keep her busy."

"I have always been surprised you did not follow in her footsteps. Very advantageous marriage with impeccable connections. Two children, boy and girl, so nicely spaced."

Then you do not know me as well as you think. Two weeks of Chrissie's locked-box world and I would be a screaming lunatic. Smile here. Do this there. Be a good girl. Ugh!

Vaughn grimaced automatically. "Chrissie and I rarely followed in each other's footsteps."

Major understatement.

"And yet there was opportunity, no doubt."

A discreet knock on the mahogany door and the entrance of Dewhurst forestalled Vaughn's response. As if she had one. Was this a test? Or an interrogation? There were currents beneath the comments, but she couldn't put her finger on them. Getting the stuffing knocked out of her made clear thinking more difficult. Another pillow to embroider. At this rate, she'd have an apartment full of pithy sayings to remind her what happened to fools who wanted to break out of their gilded cages.

Ling Mai waited until Dewhurst left and Vaughn raised the fine Sevres cup to sip before she spoke again. "How are you finding your stay with the Agency thus far?"

Ling Mai's question shifted Vaughn back to one boarding school after another. *And how do you find your stay at Pemberton? At Childings School for Fine Young Girls? At the Academy?*

There really was only one answer. She'd learned that lesson years ago. Now, as then, Vaughn smiled and nodded. "All is well."

"Is it?"

Now what did that mean? Had someone squealed

about the exchanges between her and tarot bitch? Or was it Stone? But it didn't seem to be his style to attack using another as a weapon.

"Is there something specific you want to know, Ling Mai?" Vaughn cut to the chase quicker than a proper lady would.

If her bluntness surprised the other woman, nothing showed.

"I simply want to make sure you are adjusting well." Ling Mai offered an enigmatic smile. "I know the training has been intense."

Training and trainer. Vaughn nodded. "I didn't expect it to be a piece of cake, but I'm here for the duration. I didn't come here to fail."

"Have there been any problems?"

Other than Mega Terminator Stone? And the bruises, lack of sleep, being pushed to exhaustion and beyond?

"Nothing worth mentioning." Vaughn took a slow sip of tea, savoring it across her tongue. It beat the tea bags they used in the commissary.

"And if there were, would you speak to me about them?"

Them or him?

"Of course," Vaughn lied without hesitation. One was not raised as an ambassador's daughter without learning a few of the unspoken rules.

"I see." Ling Mai nodded and Vaughn thought they understood each other perfectly.

"When do I find out the real reason behind your asking me here?" Vaughn was too tired to worry about proper etiquette. Maybe she was learning something from Stone, after all.

"You are more your father's daughter than you realize."

It wasn't the response Vaughn had expected, or wanted, not with the accompanying squeeze to the heart.

"You will not tell me, then? Is this meeting about my father? Or are you concerned about my ability to see the training through?"

"You yourself said it's been challenging."

"I won't fail, Ling Mai."

"I have always known that."

"Then what do you want? Are you going to tell me the real reason you suggested I become a recruit?"

"Not yet, my dear. It is not time. You must have patience."

"And then?"

"Then you'll be told what you need to know."

"Not until I finish training?"

There was the most imperceptible of pauses. Vaughn set down her tea as the other woman spoke.

"You are no longer a child, Vaughn. Patience is a virtue that is more hard-won for some than others."

"As is honesty."

"Ah, but I have not been dishonest with you."

Vaughn held her tongue for a change, then stood, realizing there was little being accomplished here except shadowboxing, and she wasn't even sure about that. Another side effect of the brutal training, no doubt.

"It has been pleasant, Ling Mai." Baffling as all get

out, but a nice break. "But I am required at the firing range."

"So eager to return to your lessons?"

Another tricky question, and one with no clear answer.

"I don't have the background of many of the recruits, as you well know, so I need all the training I can get."

"Though I hear that your ballet classes have held you in good stead. Your mother would be proud." Ling Mai gave another of her private smiles.

So word had already reached the director. Interesting. Probably not from Stone. Or maybe it was? She'd give a year's allowance to know the spin the instructor put on that little show. On the other hand, Ling Mai could have simply been monitoring one of the surveillance cameras tucked around the compound.

"Yes." Vaughn took a step toward the door. "Mother would be glad to know all the time and expense is finally paying off. Not quite how she hoped, I'm sure, but then I never have never done things quite as Mother had hoped."

Another major understatement.

"Take care, my dear." Ling Mai rose behind her desk. "The next weeks will be even harder than the last."

Out of the frying pan and into the fire. Good thing she liked a challenge.

"Thanks. I'll keep that in mind."

"And if you need to talk—about anything—I am here for you."

At what cost? Was it wise to show one's weaknesses,

one's fears, to the person who held the power over Vaughn's dream? Not likely.

"Thank you. I'll keep that in mind, too."

Vaughn left, nearly crashing into Stone in the hallway as she closed the door behind her.

"Interesting talk?" the instructor asked. He was standing too close, but then again, his standing anywhere in the same building was too close. From here, she could smell the scent of his skin, shower-fresh and warm. A tempting scent. Not that she planned to go there.

"Very illuminating."

"You discuss how rough you're finding it here?"

"Nah." Vaughn gave him a hundred-watt smile. "Designer clothes. Best restaurants in Paris. Whether the Bergdorf-blonde look would last long." She gave one shoulder a careless toss that hurt like hell. "You know, the usual."

He stilled and she realized she'd touched a nerve. Interesting. Slam the man on the dojo floor and it didn't faze him; sling a few catty phrases his way and he reacted. Why?

"You're late for the range."

Leave it to him to level the playing field immediately.

"Funny, that's exactly what I told Ling Mai."

"Everyone else calls her the director."

If it was meant as a rebuke, he had failed.

"I know. That's why I don't. Maybe I'll start calling you M.T."

"Try it, Monroe, and pay for it."

She only increased her smile and started humming as she strode away. Bearbaiting was outlawed in most countries in the world, but she suddenly understood its allure.

Chapter 3

"**Y**ou want to do what?" Disbelief coated Alex's words.

"You heard me. I want to visit the director's office."

"Break in, you mean?"

"Visit. Temporarily. I'll remove nothing." Vaughn slid the small packet of tools into the band of her black pants, which matched the rest of her outfit. Only it wasn't the black of a downtown New York business day; it was the darkness of stealth.

She and the other two recruits had rendezvoused in the hallway, empty at this hour of night, leading to their spartan quarters. All the others were asleep. Wise women.

Kelly stepped closer, concern pinching her expression. "It's not wise, Vaughn. If you're caught, it could be an automatic expulsion. What can be worth that?"

"The thrill?" She said it softly, but meant every word. What she didn't say was the real reason—her competitive gene, which could not be suppressed for long.

"Seriously, Vaughn," Kelly continued as if Vaughn hadn't answered. "I'm sure Jayleen didn't mean that ridiculous bet about digging up the dirt on M.T."

Vaughn looked at her, shaking her head. As a former kindergarten teacher, Kelly could sometimes be as innocent as they came; at other times, she had X-ray vision.

"Jayleen meant every word of it. Which is why she made it in front of as many recruits as possible."

"But you didn't have to snap at it like a trout to bait." Leave it to country girl Alex not to gloss over the obvious.

"Point is, I did accept it. Now I'm doing something about it."

"But what's in the director's office?"

"Personnel files." Vaughn considered face blackener, then discarded it. Hard to explain if she was stopped, coming or going. On the other hand, if she was stopped, after curfew and in a part of the compound normally off-limits, explanations were going to be the least of her worries.

"You expect to find out what M.T. means from his personnel file?" Alex didn't look as if she bought the idea. "Why don't you just ask the man?"

This time, it was Kelly who rolled her eyes. "Even

if Vaughn could get within a hundred yards of Stone without getting on his bad side, do you really think he's going to tell her?"

Vaughn nodded. "Wish me luck, ladies."

"Wait." Alex stepped forward. "You're not going alone."

Kelly soldiered to Alex's side even as Vaughn shook her head.

"I appreciate the thought." Which she did. More than they realized. "But I made the bet. I pay the price."

"And what kind of friends are we to let you go with no one guarding your back?" Alex demanded.

"Ditto." Kelly nodded, looking around her. "Give me two secs to get dressed. Alex will keep watch on the outer perimeter while I'll cover you inside the mansion."

"Guys—"

"'Nough said." Alex reached into the side pocket of her windbreaker. "Besides, now I get to try out these new mikes."

Vaughn looked at her hand. "I thought the lab said those were experimental. They're off-limits."

"Like what we're doing isn't?"

"You think the lab is going to look the other way if they find you liberated their new toys?"

"They'll be back in the shop tomorrow."

"If we make it through tonight."

"Having second thoughts, Vaughn?"

"Never." At least none she'd admit out loud. But the mission had changed dramatically. It was one thing when it was her tail, and her tail alone, on the line; now

Alex and Kelly could suffer, too, just two weeks before graduating. And all because Vaughn couldn't resist the smug taunt of Jayleen's words. Was this the price of friendship? If so, it was hefty.

"Let's go." Kelly had rejoined them, dressed all in black now.

"Fine. But it's still my mission." Vaughn would not let them get hurt. No way. "If I say cut and run, you two do exactly that. Am I clear?"

"She's beginning to sound like Stone," Alex muttered, her voice low as they crossed the darkened halls of the dorm area. "Lord save us from two of them."

"Smart mouth." Vaughn turned to her, a palm outstretched. "Hand me those mikes."

They inserted easily enough, a listening device the size of a large freckle placed just below the ear, a wrist-mounted microphone small and light enough to be all but invisible and disguised as an ordinary wristwatch. Very ordinary. They needed a Bugatti version if they were going to move in the world Vaughn moved in.

They checked the mikes twice before Vaughn nodded toward the empty courtyard. "Alex, take two o'clock. Patrols cross every fifteen minutes. Don't let them catch you."

"As if I haven't learned anything in the last seven weeks." Alex shook her head as she crab-shuffled off.

Kelly hung behind Vaughn's right shoulder.

"Once we make it through the front doors, I want you to stay put." Vaughn's breath vaporized in the cool night air.

"But—"

"That's an order, McAlister."

"But how are we getting though the doors? It's not like they're open."

Vaughn patted the fanny pack strapped across her waist. "I have a few tricks I learned before I arrived here."

"What kind of tricks? From whom?"

"Former boyfriend, and you'll see."

Vaughn darted ahead, aware that every second was critical. The sweep of a security light momentarily bathed the grounds as she dodged behind a juniper bush.

On the count of three, she slipped ahead, not stopping until she reached the Romanesque arched doorway leading into the main hall.

By the time Kelly joined her, Vaughn had her tools out, three spread at her feet, one rolling through her fingers.

"What are—"

"Picks." Vaughn crouched forward, ignoring the fear already congealing in her stomach.

"Lock picks? But why not the electronic—"

"They expect electronic devices." Vaughn turned her head to see and hear better. "They've rigged this door to withstand every electronic device made."

"But—"

"Think simple." She reached for the next size of metal pick. "The more we defend against the high-tech, the easier it is to forget the basics."

"Like picking a lock?" Kelly's tone indicated she was getting the gist of it.

"Exactly. Like picking a lock. A lost art as people rely solely on gadgets to counter other gadgets." That sounded profound enough—now if only the picks would work.

"And your former boyfriend taught you this?"

"Yes." The tumbler fell. A sweet, sweet sound. "This and a few other things."

She stepped inside the marble hallway, crossing to a keypad and punching in a sequence of numbers.

"You know the key code to this place?" Kelly was one step behind her.

"No. But I know a mathematical sequence that scrambles ninety-nine percent of the codes used. Another lesson from the beau." And if it worked, she'd have to take back half the awful things she had said about him. But only half.

A red light blinked off. They were in.

"And if this had been the one percent?"

Vaughn grinned. "Then we'd be screwed. Now stay here. Establish contact with Alex and keep low."

"But—"

"My mission, my call. Stay put." *And don't let yourself get hurt.*

"Be careful."

Vaughn gave no reply as she headed down the hall toward Ling Mai's office. This was a long shot. But if there was going to be any information on M. T. Stone, Vaughn guessed Ling Mai would keep it close at hand. Vaughn only hoped the game was worth the price. The image of Jayleen's stunned expression when Vaughn told her what the M.T. stood for guided Vaughn the last steps, her crepe-soled boots whispering on the marble floor.

The lock on the director's door was child's play. A few quick twists of the smallest pick and it clicked open. Obviously no one expected a security breach that would go this far.

Now or never.

Once inside, Vaughn closed the door gently behind her, waiting for the darkness to settle around her before she trusted herself to switch on her pen flashlight.

She raised her wrist to her mouth. "You there, Alex?"

"Copy. All clear."

"Kelly?"

"Nothing in sight."

So far, so good. If only her thumping heart and surging adrenaline would get the message. A few more moments and she'd have what she came for.

Three steps to the brocaded chair; jog to the left. Four more steps to the desk. The goal—a credenza immediately behind the director's ornate desk. It was the only logical place to keep files.

But when Vaughn reached the solid piece of furniture, the thin shaft of her flashlight highlighting its cherrywood surface, she paused.

"Damn."

She hadn't realized she'd spoken out loud until Alex's voice came over the mike. "Problem?"

"Just a little one."

Like hell it was. Who kept a tungsten lock on a

credenza and why hadn't she noticed this when she'd been in the office before?

"How little a little problem?"

"Nothing I can't figure out."

In a month or two.

On the other hand, she hadn't come this far to give up. The picks would get her only so far, and nowhere until she broke through the first set of double-digit keypad codes. She should have brought a drill.

No point in wasting time. She knelt, holding the light between her teeth and set to work. She'd almost broken through the first wall when Alex's voice came through the headset.

"Kelly, eyes open, ten o'clock."

"I see them."

Them? The ground sweepers usually walked singly.

Vaughn spoke around the flashlight in her mouth. "How many?"

Alex's voice overrode Kelly's. "Four. Headed straight for the main house."

Four? Who could have—Jayleen.

Old win-at-any-price Jayleen.

"Kelly, you and Alex clear out. Now."

The first lock opened. Choices? Try for the second or save her skin?

"No way."

"Do it. Direct order."

She leaned closer to the lock, hoping her comrades did as told. If anyone was going down for this, she wouldn't let it be them.

Two digits to go when she heard the slam of the front door.

One digit.

The lock gave. She shoved the drawer open. The sudden blaze of light overhead exposed the empty drawer. Empty except for a single piece of paper. With one sentence.

Better luck next time, princess.

He had known she was coming. Jayleen was in cahoots with Stone.

It figured that like a dumb-as-day duck, she'd waltzed into her own shooting gallery. No one to blame here except herself.

She heard rounds chambered into handguns, squared her shoulders and raised her hands.

Without turning around, she knew whose face she'd see. Stone.

Crud in a bucket.

"Got anything to say, princess?" came his slow drawl with a hint of Southern charm buried deep beneath its layers. Very deep.

She stood and turned, keeping her own voice casual. "Anyone seen my eyeliner? I lost it the first day we arrived and seven weeks is just too long to be without it."

A guard ducked his head to hide a grin. There was no such response on Stone's face.

"Call Ling Mai," he barked.

"You need not bother." The director stepped into the tense room as if this were an everyday occurrence at four in the morning. "Stone, your men will not be needed anymore. Vaughn, I suggest you take a seat."

Vaughn did as directed, aware of the pit of her stomach free-falling. Ling Mai's face gave nothing away. For once she could not say the same for Stone. He closed the door behind the last guard and stood to the left of the chair Vaughn had chosen.

It placed him at a height and strategic advantage— he could watch her but, unless she craned her neck around, she could not see his every move. Another point to the instructor.

When would she learn what a neophyte she was in this world? And would she have another chance to find out?

She kept her gaze focused on Ling Mai, who took her sweet time settling herself behind the formal desk, sparing only one quick glance at the empty drawer gaping open in the credenza.

"Is there an explanation for tonight?" she asked the two before her.

That surprised Vaughn. She expected to be in the hot seat, but the words implied judgment was still suspended.

"On a routine grounds inspection, my men and I discovered the very inept Ms. Monroe breaking and entering."

Routine inspection, her foot. And what was that *inept* line? She'd broken into the drawer.

"Not so inept if she passed three levels of our security precautions," Ling Mai remarked.

Yeah. Take that, Stone.

But now was not the time to gloat. Vaughn held her tongue. Who said she didn't know how to?

"Your explanation, Vaughn?" Ling Mai turned her inscrutable gaze fully on Vaughn.

"A bad mistake in judgment." She pressed her fingers against the grain of leather armchair rests, seeking some solace in the chair's solidity. Not that it helped. Not with the fear tap-dancing through her system.

This was the end. Any moment now Ling Mai would say the fateful words—*you're out.* Stone would crow and Vaughn's worst nightmare would unfold. She'd be a failure. Her one chance at doing something, being something, and she'd have thrown it away because of a dare.

The man behind her made a noise that coming from anyone else would have been a snort.

"You disagree, Stone? It's not a failure in judgment?"

"The woman broke into your office. Who knows what types of secrets she was hoping to steal, or what she was planning to do with them."

"You knew." Vaughn shifted enough in her chair to speak to her accuser. "You knew exactly what I was going after because you set me up."

He didn't reply. He didn't even have the decency to glance at her, except for one fire-branded look that made her glad there was a third person in the room.

"Is this true, Stone?"

"An exercise," he replied to Ling Mai. "Bait was offered, and taken, without regard for the consequences, and two team members dragged into the fiasco. Not the mark of a reliable operative."

"Vaughn?"

"I admit to taking the bait. I am responsible. The consequences were known and valued as worth the risk."

"Including the possibility of dismissal from the program?"

Everything inside her stilled. *Not yet. Please, not yet.*

Her mouth puckered into dryness so fast she could not answer. Instead, she only nodded her head, a stiff, disjointed puppet-like motion.

"And your teammates?"

If anyone paid for this, it'd be her and her alone. She cleared the lump in her throat, giving emphasis to each of her next words. "They were advised, strongly, to stay behind. None of this is their responsibility. If someone is to be removed from the program, it's me, and me alone."

"But they came with you."

Time pounded against her. Could she have been more insistent? Not told them in the first place? Her whole body was suspended. Too much was at risk here. She'd acted rashly, again, and had been nailed because of it, but she was not going to let Alex and Kelly go down with her.

"I take full responsibility for what happened tonight," she repeated, her hands curling into wedges. "No one else is to blame. No one else needs to be punished."

"But you do?" Ling Mai's voice sounded like a mother's croon, soft and melodious, not capable of breaking Vaughn's heart. Which it was doing, piece by piece.

"If you think I should be punished, I'll accept that."

"You should be out," Stone spoke behind her.

It was a constant refrain with the man.

She ignored him.

Ling Mai offered only a quick glance in his direction before she spoke again to Vaughn.

"I think it best you leave now. Return to your quarters. Punishment will be decided upon and administered at the proper time. And you will accept it as such. Is that understood?"

"Yes." Vaughn stood, by willpower alone, and turned, only to find her way blocked by Stone.

"It's not over yet, princess."

"Never thought it was." She notched her chin up with her words, using the only weapon she had left. Her disdain.

He made her step around him. Harder than it sounded with her legs so wobbly.

But she did it. Marched past him, down the hall and out into the night chill. Kelly and Alex were nowhere around.

Well, when she screwed up, she did it big-time.

It would be small comfort tomorrow.

"Well?" Ling Mai waited until she heard the sound of the main door closing.

"She got farther than I expected." M.T. remained rooted behind the chair Vaughn had vacated, his stance no less tense.

"Do I detect a note of respect?"

"She acted emotionally in the first place. Risked her life and the lives of two other trainees in the process. Used equipment from the lab without authorization."

"Equipment?"

"An experimental mike set."

"Interesting. We did not foresee this. And yet she made it past the patrolled courtyard, the outer door, my office door and into the credenza. I believe you thought she'd be stopped before the first door."

"If you want me to say you were right, don't hold your breath. She might have a few talents—"

"And abilities."

"A few tricks not taught here, including tools that haven't been used since the last century. Most picks are in museums now." His words sounded like marbles tumbling against concrete in his mouth. "But it doesn't mean she'll make a good operative. Nothing's changed there."

"It is a blind man who will not see what's before his eyes."

"Don't give me that Confucius crap, Ling Mai. I happen to know you were born and raised Methodist. You're being stubborn about her."

"As are you, M.T."

"I'm trying to save her life."

"Are you?"

He slipped from stillness to alert. "What's that supposed to mean?"

"You are the most objective of men, and yet you are not objective where Vaughn is concerned."

"She's a debutante playing a very dangerous game. If she does pass the next two weeks of training, which is questionable, she'll soon tire of the cost of this game. Better to weed her out now, before she hurts herself, or others."

"That is your assessment then?"

"Yes."

"You have seen no change, no improvement in skills or mindset since she arrived."

He paused, a very telling response for this man, his gaze focused on the wall behind her chair. "Nothing that warrants her becoming a full operative."

"And her punishment?" Ling Mai smoothed invisible dust from the surface of her desk. "For her lack of good judgment tonight."

"She should be forced from the program."

"That will not happen." At his frown, she added, "Not because of this. As you said yourself, it was a test. One she handled better than expected."

"It was a trap and she walked straight into it."

"Then I shall devise the punishment, one fitting for the crime."

He shook his head, his tone even more serious than before. "I mean it, Ling Mai. You're risking more than her life by keeping her in the program."

"I am aware of this." Her tone told him he was dismissed.

"Fine." Stone turned to leave.

"M.T."

"Yes?"

"I forgot to tell you we'll be having a visitor tomorrow."

"A VIP?"

"Director of the CIA—Thomas Werner."

Stone gave a low whistle. "I'd say that's a big VIP. What's he want?"

"To see some of the new trainees at work. Make sure Jayleen is visible."

He nodded. "No problem."

"And Vaughn."

Silence greeted her request, but she noted the tightening of his jaw. Only because she was watching for a response.

"As you wish." He turned again to leave.

"All will come clear in time." It was little enough reassurance to give the man, but it was all she had right now.

He gave her no answer as he closed the door quietly behind him.

Ling Mai glanced once more at the open drawer and the piece of paper that still lay there. Only then did she smile. One could not help the small trill of anticipation. After all, it was her father's people who had invented fireworks and there was still tomorrow. It would be interesting to watch.

Chapter 4

Vaughn expected dismissal at first light. The last thing she expected was to be called to martial arts drill as if nothing had happened. Across the dojo floor, she could see Kelly and Alex, separated from each other as they were from her, but neither looking the worse for wear.

Maybe this was a diabolical Stone torture device. Let the victims assume all was well before he sprang his punishment.

And punishment there would be; she had no doubt. Not with the look in Stone's eyes last night, nor the sideways glance he gave her this morning as she passed single file on entering the hall.

The man wanted her out of the program. Almost as

much as she wanted to remain in, and she wanted it soul-deep. She held no clue as to what had set Stone against her, almost from the start, but it'd been there, day in and day out. The taunts, the challenges, the pricking at a pride she shielded herself with when all else failed. He wanted to win, but so did she. A clash of wills, growing stronger every day.

So be it. Vaughn had heard the term *willful* applied to her more than once in her upbringing, always as a negative. Only fair that it should finally serve her in good stead now.

She moved through the opening sparring routines automatically, her breathing increasing, her heart rate pumping harder, her mind not on the lunges or the calls of *"kiyee."* Not while she waited for the sky to fall.

A quick glance upward, to the railed balcony rimming the front half of the hall, showed her several silhouettes. Ling Mai's obviously, by her height next to those who stood around her. The others were men. One to the fore, several spread out. They looked like guards. As the daughter of a former ambassador, she recognized the stances. Some children grew up with ice cream and ponies; she grew up with security precautions and protocol.

Stone called the group to attention, snapping out names to pair off. He set her against Jayleen.

Maybe the man had a sense of humor after all.

Jayleen looked wary as she approached Vaughn and bowed. She should; Vaughn wanted to beat the stuffing out of her. Slowly. Deliberately. And officially.

She might even have to thank Stone later.

Like in her next life.

"Surprised to see me?" she taunted Jayleen, who circled just out of arm's reach.

"Should I be?" Rumor had it Jayleen had come from the streets, a hardscrabble life in a dog-eat-dog world. Her tone alone told Vaughn that she hadn't survived such a background by being a lightweight. In another time and place, Vaughn might have admired what it had taken the other woman to make it thus far. But not now, and not here.

Vaughn lowered her voice and said with a grin, "Just wanted to make sure you weren't celebrating too soon."

"Celebrating?"

"Should have read those tarot cards you're always playing with, Jayleen. They might have showed you your future."

"What future?"

Vaughn didn't answer. Instead, she moved in fast and low, slamming Jayleen against the mat with a sweep of feet taking her out.

Jayleen countered by rolling. Vaughn was on her like an avalanche roaring down a mountain face, pinning her windpipe before Jayleen could utter a sound.

Seconds slowed. Adrenaline slammed through Vaughn's veins. Adrenaline and something else, something hot and primordial. Rage. Not for last night's cheap betrayal, but for what this woman had almost cost her. Still could cost her. And not only her, but also Alex and Kelly.

And Stone didn't think Vaughn had it in her to kill.

"You ever mess with my friends again and I won't stop," Vaughn whispered, her face inches away from Jayleen's.

"Monroe. Back off."

Stone bellowed his orders behind her. He no doubt sensed how close to the line she was, how easy it would be to cross over.

She inhaled a deep breath and rocked back on her heels.

"You all right?" he asked Jayleen.

"Fine, sir." It sounded like a croak.

Vaughn stood, knowing the ax would fall for sure now. It was bad form to attack and nearly choke one's teammate. No matter how justified the action.

She heard the hum of stunned voices in the dojo, where shouts and calls should have been; only the low buzz of whispers reverberated back and forth. The other trainees might not know the details of what had just happened, but all were only too aware that something was going down. Vaughn, Stone and Jayleen within touching distance meant fallout, of the barely controlled kind.

But when she glanced at Stone, his attention was directed elsewhere, to the entranceway, where a small dark cloud of people entered, their suits and ties looking out of place amongst the white *gis*.

Vaughn let her gaze follow his, the slam of recognition hitting her midgut. She stood, bracing herself with the motion.

Was this the punishment, then? The one Ling Mai said would happen when it needed to happen.

If so, she and Stone had chosen well.

"Director." Stone nodded to Ling Mai, who looked feminine and exotic among the towering men surrounding her.

She in turn smiled and waved a hand toward the silver-haired gentleman at her side. "Director Werner, I would like you to meet our chief instructor, M. T. Stone."

"Mr. Stone." The older man extended his hand in a warm and friendly handshake Vaughn recognized from a thousand different functions. Just as she noted Werner's gray eyes did not display their usual warmth, but rather a wariness that withheld judgment. But not for long.

Vaughn had to give Stone credit. It would have been easy to defer, or hesitate when dealing with the other man, who exuded a type of regal dominance. But Stone showed no servitude in gripping the other's hand. In fact it was the CIA director who looked surprised. One alpha male sizing up another.

Vaughn could have sworn she heard cymbals clashing.

Ling Mai stepped into the momentary silence. The diplomatic world had lost a real asset in not snatching her up. "And two of our students. This is Jayleen Smart."

This time, Werner did not extend his hand. "You make a worthy opponent."

"Thank you, sir."

Points to Jayleen. Vaughn recognized that subtlest of tones the older man used, one hinting at displeasure without rising a single decibel. Jayleen hadn't so much as flinched, but then maybe she wasn't tuned in to the frequency like Vaughn was.

"And this is?" the director asked, not waiting for Ling Mai to speak as he turned and extended his hand to Vaughn.

"Vaughn Monroe," came Ling Mai's reply, somewhere in the background as Vaughn simply stood there, looking at the hand, waiting for it to snap out and bite her.

Time seemed to freeze, a cold, crackling sensation blurring voices around her.

It was Stone who shifted first. It was not like him to bring attention to himself in any way. Yet she was glad he did. His movement broke the awkwardness.

The director's hand slid to his side, unshaken, as his voice sounded calm and reasonable when he repeated Ling Mai. "Monroe? An interesting name."

"My mother's maiden name." The words came automatically, too late to swallow back. But then she wasn't telling him anything he didn't already know.

"I see. And she is aware you are here?"

"No. She thinks I'm with friends in Cannes."

Currents within currents. Very dangerous currents, and Vaughn sensed them getting deeper and more treacherous with each passing second.

Ling Mai watched them closely. Vaughn also noted Stone's gaze assessing them both.

"Do you think she would approve of your choice in being here?" the director asked.

"I'm an adult. My choices are my own."

Even Jayleen started glancing between faces, trying to pinpoint the increasing tension.

"I believe it is time to move on." Ling Mai laid a hand upon the director's arm.

He glanced at it, then shrugged, not moving an inch.

It was obvious he was not finished as he spoke once more to Vaughn, first glancing at Stone. "Ask your instructor here about choices and how rarely we can claim to own them."

Vaughn had to give the man points. As a parting salvo the comment was good, straight to the gut with a double-whammy twist to the heart. But then he'd had years of practice. He nodded to Ling Mai and the group moved in unison toward the far door.

Vaughn slowly took a breath, but it did nothing for her racing heart.

"Jayleen." Stone's voice broke the web holding the trainees hostage, staring after the departing group. "Head to the showers. Practice is over."

If Jayleen meant to protest, she bit her tongue. They'd barely begun practice, yet Stone was dismissing her in a public venue.

That had to sting.

Especially as he waited until she left to address Vaughn.

"You want to tell me what that was all about?" He stepped close enough so his words, and their edge, were for her ears alone.

"It appears the CIA director was taking a tour."

She kept her gaze averted; it was easier to sustain a light tone when not impaled by Stone's look.

But he wasn't buying it. His hand came up to grasp her arm, not hurtful but hard. Even to a first-day trainee, it was apparent he wanted answers, and Vaughn was no first-day recruit.

"You're on a thin rope as it is, princess. Don't push it."

The long, sleepless night. The waiting for punishment, and envisioning a thousand forms it could take. The last five minutes. She could blame them all for the tremble of her next words, but it was more than that. Stone pushed buttons. Her buttons. The man had an unerring sense of how to get beneath her skin.

She turned so that she faced him. "What do you want me to say, Stone? Just spell it out. Then you can go your way, and I'll go mine."

For a moment he looked confused, but the man didn't do confused. Not that she'd ever seen.

"Why the questions? You know the CIA director? He one of your social connections? Why you got into this program in the first place?"

"Oh, give me a break. You've read my file, probably know more about me than I know about myself."

"If you're snowing me here, it won't work."

"What does snowing have to do—"

"Monroe, why did he ask about your mother?"

"Why shouldn't he?"

Stone looked as if he wanted to throttle her. Instead, he took a deep breath before speaking between clenched teeth.

"Who is he to you?"

"Don't be an idiot, Stone. You know he's my father."

Chapter 5

Vaughn leaned against the plush seats of her aunt Francine's stretch limousine. It was amazing what twenty-four hours could do. Yesterday, Stone had been in her face about her father; today, she was sitting across from Jayleen, Alex and Kelly, Stone's words echoing in her mind.

"This is your first field op." His look was as hard-edged and clipped as his tone as he read from a PDA. "You'll be broken into teams of four, with a team leader, an assignment and a designated time frame to complete your trial mission. Each team will have an off-site target, with details and execution the ultimate responsibility of the individual team leaders. I will be coordinating from Op Center. Each team will be given less than twelve hours to complete their mission and return here. If your mission is not completed, don't bother returning."

The man really did need to work on that nurturing aspect of his personality.

But that wasn't the pièce de résistance. Leave it to Stone to hold out until the last minute to drop his next little bomb.

"Monroe, you're team leader, with McAlister, Noziak and Smart as your team."

"Yes!" Alex gave her a high five, a nice contrast to Stone's taunting glance.

And that was when her gut twisted big-time. He expected her to fail. No doubt he was setting them all up to fail, with her leading them. A strike taking out all the players at once. The man was positively Machiavellian.

"You think you know what you're doing?" Jayleen demanded, her contempt not hidden as the large group broke up and started leaving the room.

That was a million-dollar question and one Vaughn still heard reverberating around her thoughts. This wasn't just about her and Stone; this involved the others now. Their mission—get into a small, very exclusive, very popular and public night club, retrieve a notebook from a ruthless club owner and leave with no one the wiser.

Piece of cake. Yeah, right.

"I've got to tell you," Alex said, grinning from the seat opposite Vaughn. "So far, I'll go on an ops with you any day. I like your style. And riding in this set of wheels ain't bad, either."

"I don't think Stone would approve," Jayleen interjected, brows angled and arched over her deep-set eyes, her set of tarot cards flipping through her hands without sound. A sure sign of unease.

"Well, he's not here, is he?"

Thank God. Vaughn smoothed sweaty palms down her silk stockings. If her team was aware how her stomach twisted and her neck muscles clenched, they might not be so open to her plan. One she hadn't run past Stone before she took the plunge.

"Jayleen, pull a card and give us our fortune," Alex said with a laugh, leaning forward to nudge the other woman.

"Not sure you all would want to hear the future," came the pointed response.

Fighting words, but Vaughn wasn't about to step away from battle at this point.

"Go ahead." She shrugged. "Let's see if you know as much as you think you do."

Button pushed. Point to Vaughn as Jayleen shuffled her cards forcefully, nearly crushing them. But her grin was bright, if a little tight as she fanned the deck before Vaughn.

"You pick our fortune. You're the leader."

Not in that tone of voice. Vaughn hesitated before sliding one card out, turning it face upward, its image flashing as the lights of Manhattan pulsed past the limo windows.

Damn and double damn. Vaughn didn't know one

card from another, but this one did not look good. A woman cringing against a hail of swords angled toward her from above. Not good at all.

"Seven of Swords. Opposition." Jayleen's voice couldn't have said *I told you so* any plainer.

"What's that mean?" Kelly spoke up, no doubt looking for the silver lining. They bred them optimistic in the heartland.

"Could mean all sorts of things." Jayleen kept her dark eyes on Vaughn.

"Cut the crap, Jayleen." Vaughn's tone held no humor. "I'll not have us going into our first mission and you sabotaging it with your hoodoo voodoo."

"It's not—" Jayleen squared her jaw and looked at Alex and Kelly before responding. "The Seven of Swords means you must be logical and persistent to escape from the opposition you encounter."

"That doesn't sound so bad." Alex glanced at Vaughn, who still wasn't buying any of it.

"Believe or not," Jayleen spoke directly to Vaughn. "The cards are meant to help, not harm."

"Does this card mean anything else?" Kelly asked.

Jayleen sucked in a deep breath. "It means one must face the fact that troubles are often self-created and that only by identifying them can you eliminate repeated negative patterns. By doing so you will no longer add your forces to the opposing force's energy."

"Well, I think that's a good card." Kelly smiled at the group. "In fact that sounds like something my gran would say. Not the same way, of course. She'd say,

'Get out of your own way girl, you're making things worse than they are.'"

Alex was the one who laughed first, a snort then a full-blown belly laugh. Jayleen joined in with a grin. Vaughn wished she could release enough tension to do more than smile, but too much was riding on tonight's outcome and she was responsible for all of it.

Opposing forces, her big toe. He had a name—Stone—and if Vaughn had anything to do with it, he was going to be sorely disappointed by tonight's outcome when her team returned with ledger in hand well within their twelve-hour time frame.

Aunt Francine's silver stretch limo slid to a silent stop before the snake line of partygoers and pulsing neon lines announcing the Scarlet Club on West 28th between 10th and 11th, the low thrum of Afrika Bambaataa beating its electrofunk rhythm through the muggy night.

Vaughn glanced at her team members. They looked good. Real good. Kelly in a powder blue Stella McCartney that made her resemble a forties starlet, especially with the way Alex had waved Kelly's blond hair into a Veronica Lake style. Alex looked smashing in a simple silk sapphire sheath that contrasted nicely with her copper skin and thick waist-length black hair. Very wanton seductress.

And then there was Jayleen, who actually was the most eye-catching of them all with her hip-high leather boots, black leather mini and bustier displaying her cleavage to its full advantage. Even the makeup Alex had applied to the woman fit the outfit—blood red lipstick, deep smoky eye shadow and a mole just to the left of her full lips.

"You want to explain why I'm the one who has to look like a cross between a drag queen and a vampire?" Jayleen had demanded when first shown the outfit.

"I don't think that bustier is going to give the impression of a man-wanna-be-female or a bat guy," Alex countered before Vaughn could pipe up.

"I think you look very sexy," Kelly added, smiling.

Jayleen had simply sniffed and tied and stuffed herself into the form-fitting, knock-'em-dead designer dress. She'd cornrowed her hair off her face, displaying every angle and slant to her killer visage. No doubt if they survived the night, the woman would have a dozen offers to pose for both mainstream and X-rated material.

They might all be headed for disaster, but they would be doing it dressed to the nines. Vaughn would have to remember to thank her aunt later; having connections in the fashion industry did come in handy. Another detail Stone didn't know.

Vaughn tugged the sequined Versace tube dress that split center-thigh and exposed a long line of leg, though it tended to ride too low for Vaughn's usual comfort level. Her voice held steady as she asked, "Ready, ladies?"

"Not quite." Leave it to Jayleen to be the party pooper. "I'd like a few more details to this suicide mission."

"It's simple." Vaughn kept the frustration out of her voice. "I get us in the door."

"A big if with this line." Jayleen waved at the crowd beyond the tinted glass shielding them.

"Let her finish." Alex ran her fingers across butter-soft leather seats. "Vaughn's got us this far. Let's give her a chance."

"Thank you." Vaughn nodded toward the Idaho girl, appreciating her more and more every minute. "Like I said, I get us in the front door. We find Giorgio. Get him alone in his office. Keep him occupied. Break into his safe and waltz out."

Why was it when you put some plans into words they sounded really dicey?

"Yeah, it's that part after getting through the front doors that worries me." Jayleen eyed Vaughn, then glanced at the other two. "Those details are a little scant for my liking."

"We improvise." Vaughn ratcheted up her smile and leaned toward the handle, afraid if she didn't move soon all her muscles would lock into place and Stone would be proved right—she didn't belong as an operative, especially leading a team. "Now, let's go."

The door silently slid open as Vaughn extended one Miu Miu–shod foot to the pavement. "Remember, ladies, we're a team." She glanced over her shoulder at them and added, "Smile, follow me and own it."

"Those Stone's orders or your own?" Alex grinned.

"Or more improvisation?" Jayleen murmured, loud enough for Vaughn to hear.

Instead of replying, Vaughn glided from the car, a move she'd made many times before, praying her team believed in her enough to follow, that they weren't in over their heads and that she wasn't, either.

Ignoring the throng halted by a burly bouncer who looked part WWE wrestler and part pit bull, Vaughn smiled brightly and waltzed right up to the man, laying one hand across his steel-ribbed chest.

"Ice, it's been a while," she purred.

"Miss Vaughn." He looked beyond her before his gaze slid back to hers. "Last time was Templeton's. You was with that producer dude. I haven't seen you here before."

"I've saved this place for a special occasion." She waved her free hand toward her team. "I brought some of my best friends, as a surprise for Giorgio."

"Surprise?"

She nodded her head toward Jayleen and deepened her smile before asking, "Do you think he'll like?"

"Yeah." He nodded. "What about the others?"

Opening her eyes wide, she shrugged. "Appetizers?"

The man's laugh vibrated through him like a subway train deep underground.

"I guess I'll let you in then." He moved to unfasten the silk cord, earning grumbles and complaints from the nearest patrons.

"You are a sweetheart." Vaughn rose on tiptoe to brush a kiss across his stubbly cheek. "And *soooo* very yummy."

The man's grin assured her that he didn't have a clue what was going down. First step accomplished. If only the next phase moved as smoothly.

She breezed past him and stepped into the dim, pulse-pounding interior.

"What was that all about? Another ex-boyfriend?" Jayleen asked as they drew together inside the main foyer, a small anteroom opening to a packed dance floor with scarlet strobe lights giving everything the look of a vampire orgy.

"No. A friend, something you might want to learn how to cultivate. I got us in." Vaughn scanned the area in front of her. "If we used Stone's plan we'd be waiting in that line until after our time frame expired."

"Good move." Alex moved up close on her other side, winking at an Armani male model giving her the once-over. "Fun place. What now?"

"Improvise." Vaughn hoped it'd be enough. "Giorgio no doubt has a room in the back or on an upper level. Let's find it."

"I'm not sure I can do this." Kelly leaned toward Vaughn, her voice a raw whisper, her glance darting around the room. "They have nothing like this in Kansas."

That was the challenge to the team concept. If one member failed, they all failed, and Stone would win. Which wasn't an option.

"Kelly, I believe in you. Alex believes in you. Jayleen is guarding your back." In theory at least, but Vaughn would skip over that detail. "And Ling Mai believes in you, or you wouldn't be here. So now it's up to you. We go forward as a team or we turn around and kiss this mission goodbye."

Vaughn watched as the kindergarten teacher swallowed hard and nodded. "You lead. I'll follow," she said, angling her head upward.

Good. Another hurdle surmounted.

"I just want to know one thing." Jayleen held her ground, letting other patrons wash around her.

"What now?" Vaughn asked in exasperation.

Jayleen glared at her, lights making her appear more exotic and dangerous than usual. "Where's our backup plan, if this *improvisation* of yours goes south? Bigtime."

"We run like hell." Vaughn ratcheted up her plastic smile. "Ladies, let's go."

Bumping and grinding their way across the packed floor Vaughn was sure she'd lost Kelly once or twice. The blonde had no sense of survival as one patron after another, both male and female, snagged her into formhugging, skin-rubbing dance moves. Definitely not the Kansas two-step.

Vaughn finally leaned over the openmouthed Kelly and shouted to be heard over the music. "Pretend you're getting your class to the bathrooms. They all need to get there ASAP. And together. No stopping, no getting distracted. Now think about the team. Got it?"

The other woman gave her a sheepish smile. "Sorry. It's a first."

And was going to be a last if they didn't get to Giorgio's and get that ledger.

Vaughn nodded and pushed forward, following Jayleen's lead. Now there was a woman who could hold her own on a dance floor, impervious to the sensation she created brushing her way through the throng. The woman let nothing stop her. Now it was only a question of whether she'd hold fast for the team, as well.

Vaughn would deal with that if or when it came up; for now, the focus was on reaching Giorgio's office. For a second, Vaughn hesitated, wondering if maybe Stone's plan to reconnoiter the club as patrons first, then wait until after the club closed and do a little after-hours B and E might have more merit than she'd originally given it. Then she brushed the thought aside. Now was not the time to get cold feet. Now was the time to be brazen. Well-behaved women rarely made history.

It was Alex, though, who took the lead once they reached the solid oak door at the far end of the dance floor. The door was guarded by not one but two bruisers who made Ice outside look like a playground bully.

Alex shimmied right up to them, took a cue from Vaughn's earlier example and greeted them like long-lost friends.

"Hey, boys," she cooed, as if she did it every night of the week, rubbing up against the nearest refrigerator. "I've got a big surprise for your boss man."

"Go away," the monster growled.

"And have to tell Giorgio later that you wouldn't let us through?"

Vaughn watched one guard trade glances with the other. The first chink.

Alex responded by shaking her waterfall of straight, dark hair with one hand while sucking an index finger as a lollipop, her attention still on the barbarian guarding the gate.

She definitely had everyone's attention now, especially Kelly's. Vaughn was glad for the dark shadows, otherwise Kelly's face would be glowing with a neon blush. Even Jayleen's eyes were wider than usual.

"What you want?" the first guard asked, his voice huskier than a moment ago.

"To surprise Giorgio," came Alex's low, throaty response. Man oh man, whatever they taught those cowgirls out in Idaho, it held a mighty powerful kick.

"You need four of youse to do it?"

"She-Ra here gets first dibs." Alex angled her head toward Jayleen. "Then Chicky Boom Boom. Then me."

Vaughn swallowed a groan. She was Chicky Boom Boom? Her mother would have been appalled. On the other hand, it was much better than Stone's tag.

"And her?" The guard squinted at Kelly.

Alex released a laugh a full octave lower than her speaking voice before answering. "Oh, she likes to watch."

Vaughn ducked her head, but not before she saw the big guy's jaw drop.

Alex deserved an Academy Award for this. And if they made it out in one piece, Vaughn just might have to make a few calls to get her one. Or at least a facsimile.

"The boss know you're here?" The second guard sidled up, obviously the brighter of the two, or the less distracted.

"I told you, it's a surprise." Then, to seal the deal,

Alex released a soul-deep sigh and turned toward Vaughn. "Come on, if these boys don't know what they're missing we can always play elsewhere."

"Wait." The first guard shuffled his feet before asking, "What's in it for us?"

At Jayleen's groan, he added, "I mean, in case the boss is miffed. It could cost us our jobs, us letting you in there without an invite."

"You'll get to watch the video." It was Kelly who stepped forward, looking like the kindergarten teacher she was, and flooring them all.

"Video?" came the squeak.

"Yup. We'll make you your own *hard* copy."

The first guard nodded his head like a bobble head. They were in.

We just might pull this off. Take that, Stone, put it in your pipe and smoke it.

Vaughn led the way as the door opened, spying Giorgio behind a Danish Modern cherrywood desk, talking into a cell phone.

"What the—"

"Shh, it's a surprise." Vaughn circled around behind him so he could get a full view of her team, and Jayleen in particular, who slid into the room, the door closing silently behind them.

Giorgio looked like other nightclub owners and managers Vaughn had met over the years. Slicked-back hair, Armani suit, muscles kept in shape from a membership in an exclusive gym and just a shade of seediness around the edges. With Giorgio, it showed in the lines bracketing his eyes. Harsh lines shadowing cold orbs. This was not a man one would want as an enemy.

"Hello, big boy." Jayleen formed her lips in a sin-red lipstick pout, draping forward across the desk until her boobs all but burst from the bustier. "We're here for some fun."

Giorgio snapped his phone closed and started to stand up, but Vaughn already had her hands twined around his neck. A lover's embrace, or at least that was what she hoped he remembered. Reaching the vagus nerve slightly below his Adam's apple, she applied a firm pinch.

The man slumped backward, dead weight as Vaughn maneuvered him back into his leather swivel chair.

"Wow, how'd you learn to do that?" Alex whistled, crossing around the desk to help.

"A boyfriend who was a former SEAL."

"Cool. How long will it last?"

"Not long. Jayleen, you have the stuff?"

"'Course I do." Jayleen stepped forward and deftly inserted a needle into the vein of the man's right arm. At Kelly's wide-eyed look, she muttered, "What? I learned a few tricks on the street. This stuff will have him sleeping for just enough time for us to get in and do our stuff. He won't even know what hit him."

Vaughn glanced to where Kelly still stood by the door, glad Jayleen wasn't squeamish about needles and veins. "Kelly, you listen at the door in case those bouncers get curious. Jayleen, when you're done, you and Alex make Giorgio here look like he's been having a good time. When he wakes we don't want him to have a clue what happened."

"And you?" Jayleen asked, even as she finished and started tugging Giorgio's necktie and shirttail loose.

"I'll get the ledger."

Wall safe seemed the best bet. It took her less than fifteen seconds to find it, thanking heaven that it was an older tumbler brand, and set to work.

By the time she'd finished pulling out a small ledger and turned around, Jayleen had Giorgio's pants unzipped, his shirttail dangling, and Alex was applying a tube of lipstick along the hem.

"What—oh, smart idea." Vaughn had to give the two women credit; they were inventive.

"Got it?" Alex capped her lipstick and straightened.

"Yeah. Ready to go?"

"How we going to get a ledger out of here without the goons noticing?" Jayleen asked. "None of these dresses leave a lot to the imagination."

She had a point.

But before Vaughn could come up with a solution, Jayleen started untying the top strings to her bustier and grabbed the ledger, stuffing it along her lower back.

"There." She grinned, looking up and answering Kelly's quizzical expression. "Let's face it, no one's looking at my backside."

Another good point.

Leaving a still dazed Giorgio slumped in his chair, they sauntered out of the room, left instructions with the bodyguards to give their boss a few minutes to recuperate, gave them a blank surveillance video they'd found inside the office and exited the club.

It wasn't until they reached the limo and were once again inside it that Alex let out a war whoop.

"We did it! We're one hell of a team."

Vaughn's sentiments exactly.

She just hoped Ling Mai—and Stone—agreed.

Chapter 6

"Do you have any idea of the risk you took? Of the risk you put your team in?" Stone's voice crashed against her, a wall of icy rage, stronger for the control she heard in its depths. "The guards had weapons."

"They didn't use them."

"There were hundreds of civilians who could have been at risk if events backfired."

"They didn't. No bullets, no blood."

"Giorgio can ID you to the authorities if he recognized your face."

"He didn't." Not that she had given him much of a chance. "Besides, what's he going to say? Some society deb waltzed in there and stole a ledger. He'd be the laughingstock of the city."

"And what if he decides to pursue private retaliation?"

"Are you angry because we completed the mission or because we didn't fail?" she shot back, tired, exhausted and no longer quite so afraid that this man could sabotage her plans. Not when her team was the only team to have completed their assignment successfully.

But now it was only Stone and herself in Ling Mai's office, waiting for the director in spite of the late hour, Vaughn still wearing her Versace. An outfit that showed way too much skin and seduction for her peace of mind. Stone had given her one hot, slow look that still had her nerve endings jangling before he announced an emergency meeting—Vaughn, himself and Ling Mai, while the rest of her team waited outside closed doors.

What was it Jayleen had said? *Troubles are often self-created and only by identifying them can you eliminate repeated negative patterns.* So how did one eliminate Stone?

It was inevitable that he wouldn't have approved of her means to accomplish her mission, if for no other reason than that she was team leader, but she hadn't quite expected the extent of his anger. She wasn't sure why, either. She'd snagged the ledger. Her team had come back in one piece. What more did the man want?

But she wasn't going to let him win at this point. She'd taken a major step along the path to her dream. Hers and hers alone. Not her father's, not her mother's, not her society peers'.

Stone was wrong. Her parents were wrong. She did have something to give, to offer.

She'd lived in that other world already—glitzy, glamorous nothingness—and she wasn't going back. No matter what Ling Mai said. No matter what Stone or her father wanted. She was here, and here she was going to stay.

When Ling Mai opened the door, Vaughn found her heart pumping fast and furious, primed to fight.

Stone wasn't going to win. She was. And she'd use every weapon at her disposal to see that it happened.

"Vaughn. Stone." Ling Mai graciously inclined her head to the pair as if they weren't standing there breathing fire between them. "Congratulations, Vaughn, on your team's performance tonight."

Score one for Vaughn's side.

But Ling Mai wasn't finished. "Vaughn, if you don't mind, would you step outside with your team for a moment? I have something to discuss with Stone."

That quickly, Vaughn's fears slammed home.

Ling Mai waited for M.T. to absorb the info she'd just relayed to him. She'd known he wasn't going to like what she had to impart, and she was right. A clock chimed five o'clock in the main foyer. Neither of them paid any attention to it.

"No way." Stone stepped forward. "You're not sending a newbie operative into a setup of this caliber. The minute something goes wrong, it's suicide."

"I agree," said Ling Mai. "It would be too danger-ous."

"So what—"

"Which is why I'm sending you along with her, M.T."

He shook his head, his lips compressed rigidly together.

"I repeat, it's suicide, Ling Mai, and you know it."

"I admit the chances are not high, but only if there is a problem."

"Yet you're sending her in anyway."

"There are not a lot of options here. You and I are both professionals. We know the risks. We must weigh those risks against the greater good."

"You've known her since she was a child."

He thrust the blade of his words and twisted it. It was what made him one of the best.

"There is no choice," she repeated.

"There's always a choice."

"Not in this case." She needed him to understand. "This is an opportunity we can't pass up here, M.T., and there's always the chance it's as simple an op as it orig-inally sounds."

"You know better than that."

"I know that if we're going to make this Agency viable, we've got to grasp the opportunities that come knocking. Interpol and the CIA have their hands tied on this mission. We don't. Not only that, we have an asset they do not."

"Monroe." His tone sounded as strained as his ex-pression.

"Yes," Ling Mai repeated. "We have Vaughn. And you."

"Does she know any of this?"

"I wanted your approval first."

"You won't get my approval." He backed away from the desk. "You have my cooperation, but only because it's the only chance the deb's got."

"Fine. I'll take it." She released a sigh and cleared her throat. "You and Vaughn will be First Team."

"Decoys?"

"Black cover."

"No fallback."

"Nothing except your own ingenuity."

"She has none."

"You are not giving her enough credit. She almost finished the gauntlet her second week here and managed to break into this office. And tonight—"

"Tonight was pure luck."

"Luck is not a commodity to sneeze at in this business."

"Luck will still get her killed in the field."

"Which is why you'll be along."

His smile was laced with bitterness. "I won't have another's unnecessary blood on my hands."

"Then make sure she stays alive."

"You're asking for a lot here."

"Yes. If we have to move on to stage two without you, I give her less than a five percent return rate if things turn dicey. With you, perhaps thirty."

"You'll accept a seventy percent failure option?"

"In this case, yes."

He stepped back and straightened, his eyes no less haunted than they had been moments ago.

"And if I say no?" he asked, his voice quiet and even.

"She goes alone."

"Does she know you want her dead?"

"On the contrary, M.T., her death is not the issue here. It is whether she retrieves the information we need."

How many times must she repeat the phrase before it became real?

"For God and country?" His tone rang as cynical as his expression.

"There is no *God* in this equation. You learned that lesson long ago."

He did not reply but turned, his back as coldly rigid as his name.

She shook her head. It was as much as she was going to get at this time. She'd have to take what he was willing to give and work with it.

"Please call Vaughn and her team back into the room."

Vaughn told herself it was lack of sleep unsettling her stomach, but at this rate she was either on her way to a serious ulcer or needed to find a way to deal with one of the drawbacks to her new career—chronic stress.

She glanced around the room, surprised to see another woman present with her original team—another new recruit, known as Mandy. A woman who wore her South American ancestry in the golden sheen of her skin, her thick mane of obsidian hair. Different than Alex, though, but maybe that was the woman's demeanor. This woman held herself still, watching, as if she were weighing options, and already had her escape route memorized.

Vaughn wondered at the recruit's presence, but only momentarily. One didn't focus on the minor when a man like Stone dominated the room, looking no more pleased than when she'd left less than ten minutes ago. Not a good sign.

"Good, we're all here," Ling Mai said in greeting.

Vaughn didn't accept the pleasant tone at face value. She sat up straighter in her chair. How many ops did it take Stone to learn that rigid exterior control? Or was he born with it?

"Before we continue, I'd like to congratulate you all on a job well done in New York this evening. Unbeknownst to the four team members, Mandy was present at the Scarlet Club and her report complements our other intel as to the success of the operation."

Vaughn caught Alex and Kelly eyeing the other woman. Jayleen gave nothing away; not even her hands moved over her cards. A lesson she must have learned living on the streets.

Ling Mai cleared her throat discreetly and continued. "Mandy will be joining the team on your first official assignment."

They were going to be trusted with a real operation. No more tests; it was showtime.

Alex's grin lit up the room while Vaughn kept her own reaction inside, a warm glow and internal high five of pleasure.

Take that, Stone!

"We're looking at a simple reconnaissance mission," Ling Mai said. "But do not delude yourself that simple means without risk."

Vaughn noted the other woman kept her gaze averted from Stone's. Something was up; it didn't take a diplomat's daughter to register the dissension between director and instructor. But why?

Ling Mai passed a series of files to Jayleen to distribute. She waited until all had them before she spoke. "This is Vladimir Nikolai Aleksandrovich Golumokoff."

As Vaughn opened her file, the name and the full-face photo registered simultaneously and her heart plummeted. A free fall straight through the Persian carpet bracketing the floor. From the corner of her eye, she caught Stone watching her.

He knew. He was waiting for some reaction from her. Too bad. She'd have to be able to breathe to react and that wasn't happening.

She glued her gaze to the photo, buying a few precious seconds to find her footing. Maybe there was some mistake? Yeah, like there'd be two Blade Golumokoffs in the world.

Ling Mai's voice slipped through Vaughn's shock.

"Mr. Golumokoff is a Russian national now living in Jakarta, Singapore, Lake Como and Belgrade."

"He's hot." Alex whistled, earning a frown from Jayleen.

"He is our target," Ling Mai continued as if Alex had

not interrupted. "He directly controls several highly lucrative international operations dealing in arms, technology brokering and white slavery."

That didn't sound like the Blade she remembered. His family, yes, but not Blade.

"At least he's not gay," Alex murmured. "The cute ones always are."

No, Blade was anything but gay, unless one used the old definition of gay—charming, suave and very, very sexy. The tug of a grin pulled at Vaughn until she caught Stone's glance and automatically suppressed the response.

Ling Mai continued, "In spite of Mr. Golumokoff's physical attributes—and he is known as a lady's man— he's a ruthless adversary. While he lets his entourage do most of his dirty work, rumor has it he's not opposed to torturing and killing."

Vaughn ignored the goose bumps crawling down her neck. This did not sound like the Blade she remembered, not at all.

Ling Mai used the term *rumor.* Meaning unsubstantiated gossip. Blade could be ruthless, no doubt, but a killer? It seemed beyond his freewheeling, fun-loving lifestyle, one that mimicked her own, until just recently. People, a lot of people, had been wrong about her; could the same be said about Blade?

"Does he have something you want?" Kelly asked, getting the group nicely back on track and forestalling any more of Vaughn's inner questions.

"This is where it becomes complicated." Ling Mai

gave a soft smile, but Vaughn wasn't fooled. The woman could play down and dirty with the best.

Ling Mai proceeded. "It appears that Golumokoff is setting up an auction at the Brighton Hall resort in Mashobra, India."

"An auction?" Jayleen's voice asked incredulously. "You mean like eBay?"

"Yes." Ling Mai raised her gaze and looked directly at Vaughn. "Only on a different scope. Vaughn, what can you tell us about Mr. Golumokoff's auctions?"

"Wait." Jayleen turned in her seat to stare at Vaughn. "You know this guy?"

Ling Mai answered before Vaughn could find enough spit to wet her throat. "Vaughn has a previous acquaintance with Mr. Golumokoff."

Every gaze swiveled her way, some speculative, one downright hostile. Talk about the hot seat.

"By acquaintance, you mean lover?" Jayleen smirked.

"No. Friend. Of sorts." That sounded lame, even to Vaughn.

"You sly dog, you." Alex offered her a wink. "I wish my old boyfriends looked like this guy."

"But I bet your old boyfriends didn't have rap sheets," Jayleen said.

"Wouldn't count on it." Alex gave Vaughn a thumbs-up before adding, "So what kind of auction?"

"Blade liked to—"

"Blade?" Leave it to Stone to stop her.

"Yes. No one calls him Vladimir. To his friends, he is simply Blade."

"Because he likes to use one?" Stone asked.

"No, because it's a diminutive of Vladimir. His family has called him Blade since childhood."

"And to his enemies?" He arched one eyebrow.

"I wouldn't know."

Ling Mai cleared her throat. "Vaughn, please tell us about Mr. Golumokoff and the auctions."

"You want to know about Blade personally?"

"Yes."

"There's not much to tell. He tends to be superstitious, has an ego the size of Texas and, when he wants to be, he can be quite charming." Something Stone could learn.

"And the auctions?" Ling Mai smiled.

"What do you want to know?" Vaughn squeezed her hands together, a little like forestalling an ejection from a carnival ride by holding tight the only thing close and stable. Where had this come from? How much did they know?

"You have been friends for some time?" Ling Mai prompted.

"Yes. Though it was always casual." That was for Jayleen's benefit. And Stone's. "And it's been a few years since our paths have crossed."

Vaughn found her thoughts casting wildly about. Images of dark-haired, world-weary Blade laughing against a sunset on Bali; the opera in Milan; late-night pints at a London pub near the British Museum. Edgy, cynical, dangerous Blade. So enticing to a much younger Vaughn, but even then she had enough common sense to know that she danced too close to a dangerous flame. He'd always been a friend, though, and at one time a close one. Yes, he might have walked a razor edge between legal and not-so-legal, but Blade was not a criminal. He was simply a man who craved action, excitement and diversion.

"The auctions, Monroe?" Stone's voice was not neutral like Ling Mai's.

"He created the auctions as a sort of game. A reason to hold private parties in odd places around the world and the auctions were the carrots dangled before very wealthy, very jaded collectors."

"What kinds of items were auctioned?" Stone continued to ask the hard questions.

"It depended."

"On what?" The man's tone was as granite-edged as his name.

"I don't know." The man did know she had nothing to do with setting up the auctions, didn't he? "On what Blade was able to find to auction. Who he wanted to be present. All sorts of issues."

"Did he auction stolen goods?"

"I didn't say that." Walk carefully; international fencing carried a hefty price tag. "Part of the allure was that these were one-of-a-kind items that would not appear by more traditional means. That was part of the temptation Blade offered. Walking the thin line between legal and not-so-legal."

"And where did you walk?" Stone's tone whispered like an icy wind through the room.

Ling Mai raised one hand. "I prefer you to tell us about the types of items you saw auctioned, Vaughn. Do you recall anything in particular?"

"A rare Chinese Han bronze. An oil attributed to Van Gogh and last seen prior to World War Two. A sapphire and ruby necklace said to have been owned by Empress Josephine. Nothing without a provenance."

"And the buyers?" Ling Mai asked.

"Only first names were used, and sometimes proxies."

"What's a proxy?" Alex asked.

"If you couldn't attend in person, Blade would let a proxy stand in. Since the auctions could last from several days to over a week, timing impacted some buyers. There were kings and politicians who could not be away for that period of time. The same with some other well-known personalities who did not want their faces seen in such a setting."

"But Blade always knows the attendees, is that correct?" Ling Mai asked.

"Yes. He never allowed anyone in without having them thoroughly vetted beforehand. To him, the auctions were part party, part power trip, part game playing."

"Meaning?" Alex leaned forward in her chair.

"Collectors of the rare and unusual could be very appreciative to be able to add to their collections. Sort of an 'I'll scratch your back if you'll scratch mine' attitude. I have no doubt Blade used some of their passions as weapons of a non-lethal sort down the road. If not overtly, then covertly."

"And how many auctions did you attend?" Stone asked.

"Two."

As if he and Ling Mai didn't already know.

"As a buyer?"

"No. Not all attendees were buyers. Blade liked to flavor the group with a variety of personalities. He said that by making the mix of people eclectic, it stimulated the competitive spirit of the buyers."

"I just bet it did. And your being related to an ex–U.S. ambassador and current CIA director—how did your boyfriend deal with that?"

"He wasn't my boyfriend and he was well aware of my father's career." She swallowed before continuing, "As I've already said, Blade liked dancing along the thin edge of a sword. I was aware my being present at an in-appropriate auction could result in a backlash against my father, as Blade was also aware my presence could land him in a lot of trouble if I used my knowledge. But he never put me at risk."

"Meaning?"

"Meaning, the auctions I attended were clean. No stolen antiquities, everything aboveboard, if border-line."

"Not very far aboveboard," Stone clarified, as if the words were needed.

The man was a cynic. But now wasn't the time to focus on Stone, not when Ling Mai wielded the power behind the operation. It was time to turn the tables and start asking questions instead of being on the receiving end.

"Is Blade auctioning something in particular you want the team to go after?" Vaughn looked directly at Ling Mai.

The older woman nodded, tapping her closed folder once before answering. "Thus far, Mr. Golumokoff's auctions have been limited to fine art, ethnographic material and jewels. Nothing very earthshaking, if skimming the edge of the law. But recently we learned of intel that does disturb us."

And that quickly Vaughn's pulse trembled into overdrive.

Ling Mai continued, "Rumors are circulating that another auction is coming, the one at Brighton Hall. A very private, very high-stakes auction with a different crowd of attendees from Mr. Golumokoff's usual auctions."

"We're to infiltrate the auction?" Vaughn spoke around the wedge in her throat.

Ling Mai paused. "If need be, we will infiltrate the auction, identify the item or items to be sold and report. Hopefully, we will not need to go that far."

Well, the mission didn't sound too dicey. Yet.

"So you're hoping Vaughn can meet up with this hunk here, find out what he's auctioning and then what?" Alex spread her hands wide.

"We're planning on her meeting with Mr. Golumokoff prior to the start of the official auction and, based on their past acquaintance, seeing if she can discover exactly what's being auctioned," Ling Mai replied.

"And if she can't?" asked Kelly.

"Then we hope she can procure an invitation to the official auction at Brighton Hall."

So why did Stone look like a tornado cloud on the horizon?

Leave it to Jayleen to say what everyone else tiptoed around. "So, worst-case scenario, if Vaughn can't get the info you want by playing footsy with this Russian, we go as a team to where he's staying and find out what's up. That's it?" Jayleen asked.

Vaughn replied before Ling Mai could. "Brighton Hall is not just a hotel. It's a luxury resort located in the foothills of the Himalayas. It's eight thousand feet above its nearest neighbors and very isolated, which is what its guests pay for."

"Precisely." Ling Mai nodded. "But hopefully we will not be required to go to Brighton Hall where Golumokoff has reserved all eighty-five rooms for his guests."

"So what do we do? Exactly? And where?" The vagueness was getting to Vaughn, as was Stone's scowl.

"As we speak, Mr. Golumokoff is arriving in Simla, the capital of Himachal Pradesh in northern India, prior to moving on to Brighton Hall. It is assumed several of the eventual auction guests will be joining him in Simla. Our mission will be to make contact with him there and determine what is being auctioned and who might be the buyers."

That didn't sound too bad. Vaughn inhaled her first deep breath since she entered the room. Until Jayleen piped up.

"And if Monroe can't squirrel the info out of her old lover?"

"Friend, not—"

"Then we find a way to get invited to the auction and get the intel there," Stone cut in. "But that's a far more dangerous proposition."

Great. Obviously, Vaughn had breathed too soon.

"But that's not likely." Kelly looked from Stone to Vaughn, a frown darkening her features. "I mean, the real mission is to see what we can do before this Russian gets to the auction location, right?"

"Correct." Ling Mai's gaze slipped to Vaughn, but it was Stone who spoke next.

"We'll be working on the principle that Monroe here can access intel that several international agencies have been unable to ascertain." Leave it to Stone to cut to the chase and leave everyone silent and looking as if all the air had been sucked out of the room.

"If she is unable to, and Golumokoff moves on to Brighton Hall without her, a location created to be isolated, inhospitable to outsiders and safe from assault, the mission is a failure. No one who is not meant to be in that resort will be there, particularly if Golumokoff uses a facial recognition program to scan not only all guests but all on-site workers for positive verification."

"So Vaughn must get the information before the auction begins." Kelly said it as a given, for which Vaughn wanted to hug her if she could move leaden limbs.

"So how does she do that? You want Vaughn to approach this man alone?" Alex asked.

"No." It was Stone who answered. "I'll be with her."

Vaughn watched Alex and Kelly exchange glances before Alex broke the awkward silence. "No disrespect intended, but I thought the point was this guy wasn't going to let any strangers into this auction thing of his. Why would he let you in?"

"Because I'll be going as Monroe's husband."

Chapter 7

Talk about your bombs being detonated in small, enclosed spaces.

Vaughn broke the weighted silence first. "It won't ever work."

"Why not?"

She glanced at tight-lipped Stone, then at Ling Mai.

As if she had time to list the thousand and one reasons. So she started with the easiest. "Because there's no need to create a sham marriage for me to approach Blade. It'd actually be easier without Stone around." She waved her hand to indicate Stone and left the obvious unstated—getting info from a man was not easy with another man hovering in the vicinity. It was that simple.

Ling Mai nodded toward Stone. "M.T.'s presence as your husband is a backup measure in case you need to attend the auction itself."

So the director didn't have a whole lot of faith in Vaughn's ability to extract intel in the first place. Nothing like a vote of confidence right off the bat.

Then there was that other issue, the real problem of playing the role of the little wife in Stone's caveman presence.

Vaughn steeled herself for speaking the truth, hoping it didn't mean she'd be kicked off the team before their first mission ever commenced.

"Fine." She kept her gaze locked on Ling Mai. "But what about the fact that no one who's seen the two of us in the same room would ever believe that we'd be a couple of any kind, much less married?"

Stone didn't even glance her way.

She waited for a response from Ling Mai, so she didn't see Stone move. One minute he was a safe distance across the room, the next he was pulling her out of her chair.

"What—"

Her protest was cut short as one of his hands circled around her waist, pulling her close, while the other threaded itself in her hair, tipping her head back.

Then his lips slid over hers.

Just like that, he was there. Hard against her, claiming and branding and tasting and asking before she could think.

Or breathe.

Or protest.

She was drowning before she'd even seen the tidal wave hit. And boy, did it hit. Wave after wave of pleasure, temptation and sweet, sinful seduction.

And then he raised his head, a few inches, staring into her eyes, his own hot and heavy-lidded, the skin stretched taut across his face, the curve of his lips snagging her whole attention.

Someone in the room sighed. And the spell broke.

Ice water against heated flesh.

His eyes became wary and watchful once again. His breathing remained calm and controlled while she gulped for air.

The man had played her for a fool in a room of her peers, but she couldn't stop her heart from pounding or unfog her brain long enough to tell him where he could shove it.

Ling Mai cleared her throat. "Any other questions?"

Stone released her and stepped back while Vaughn stood there. Simply stood there. A blind, bloody ninny.

"Then Vaughn and Stone will be the primary insertion team, due to leave in twenty-four hours for Simla. Kelly will be inserted into the same hotel as a kindergarten teacher on sabbatical."

Kelly grinned and nodded. "Great. I can act that part."

"Alex will be in the field near Brighton Hall."

Alex looked up. "But I thought we wouldn't be going to the second location."

"Backup contingency," Ling Mai explained. "It's better to be prepared than to scramble after the fact."

"Are we talking jungle here?" Alex's voice rose slightly.

Ling Mai offered a reassuring smile. "The Hall is located in the foothills of the Himalayas. Pine trees, vegetation closer to parts of Colorado or—"

"Idaho?" the beautician said, referring to her home state.

"Yes. The northern area of Idaho."

"No problem, then." Alex sat back in her chair. "Even though I'm from the southern part, I know how to function in a forest. I'll be wherever Vaughn and Stone need me to be."

"Good." Ling Mai glanced at the remaining two recruits. "Jayleen and Mandy will be the secondary team, stationed within an hour of Vaughn and Stone. As a pair, they will be responsible for tactical issues on the ground. Transportation needs, setting up a safe house in case it's needed, other details."

"Not a problem," came Jayleen's quick reply. "If it's in a city I can do it, find it, secure it."

Easy enough for everyone else to accept their job assignments. None of them were being paired with Stone, or played for a fool.

"And what will I be doing in the hotel?" Kelly looked up from her folder.

"Profiling the other guests. You will need to identify anything that will help us anticipate not only Golumokoff's motivations and next actions, but those of the other guests at the auction."

Kelly nodded.

All this took less than five minutes to transpire, but for Vaughn it was a lifetime. The others kept their gazes averted from hers, which was just as well. The last thing a fool needed was more public acknowledgment of how stupid she could be.

Ling Mai eyed the recruits.

"This may not sound like a large mission, but it is vital for a number of reasons." Her glance took in the whole group. "The skills you've learned over the last weeks are backup measures. It is hoped you will never need to use most of them on this assignment."

Guns. Knives. Pressure points to immobilize or kill. In one way, Vaughn was thankful. She didn't want to see any of her new friends, her teammates, hurt or put in danger. On the other hand, the mission sounded like child's play. Make contact with Blade, talk to him, find out what was happening. So why the wary glances between Stone and Ling Mai? Why the sham of a being married to Stone? Why couldn't one of her father's people do this?

Ling Mai continued, "I want you all to remember that one of your greatest assets as a team is your cloak of invisibility. You are trained as agents, but you are also real women with abilities and talents that you need not forget you possess."

"What about Stone?" Kelly looked at the instructor. "What's his cover going to be, besides being married to Vaughn?"

"Good question." Ling Mai glanced toward Stone. "Fortunately, when M.T. was a field op we created a very strong, very deep cover for him as an import/export merchant."

"Like in trinkets from China?" Jayleen asked.

"More along the lines of ammunition and arms. He has quite a reputation in the field, and we think it will still serve us well. I'm sure Mr. Golumokoff will be quite aware of M.T.'s cover story."

Great. Not only was she going to pretend to get married, she was marrying an international criminal. Life was just getting better and better.

"Vaughn won't be too invisible in her role," Alex pointed out. "Isn't she going to stand out?"

"Initially she will be as invisible as any of you going about your daily lives, as she'll be just what Mr. Golu-mokoff expects to see. An old friend, nothing else. Like the rest of you, her real-life role will hide her true intentions from those who are not astute enough to look beneath the external. Is this clear?"

Several heads nodded. Vaughn remained frozen in place, not yet ready to hear a pep talk, especially one that cut so close to the bone. She had expected challenges to becoming a full-fledged operative, but she hadn't anticipated having her past dug up and callously used as a stepping-stone to her future.

Jayleen's tarot reading echoed in her mind. *Troubles are often self-created and only by identifying them can you eliminate repeated negative patterns.*

In this case, she did create her own repeated pattern. The fact was that it wasn't any of the skills she'd learned over the last weeks, nor her determination, nor her innate abilities that were giving her the opportunity she'd always wanted. No, it was her connection to a man from her past. One who had been as attracted to her position as the daughter of a powerful man as he was attracted to her as a woman.

Ling Mai and Stone were using Vaughn as a pawn, nothing more.

No wonder Stone treated her as an interloper. He understood what she was only beginning to comprehend, that becoming an operative was less about her becoming the person she was meant to become and more about manipulation. And it stung. Bone-deep burned, and there wasn't a thing she could do about the pain except walk away. Which would also mean walking away from her dream.

Ling Mai closed the file in front of her. "If we're all clear about our roles, then we'll proceed. This mission will be called Red. Code Red. If it proceeds and achieves its objective in identifying both the item to be auctioned and the players involved in the auction, it will be a success and there will be more opportunities for the Invisible Recruits. Tomorrow, we'll leave for the Hamptons, where we'll stage a very public wedding for the purpose of reinforcing M.T. and Vaughn's cover. Until we meet to leave, you're dismissed."

One by one, the team stood and walked from the room until only Vaughn, Stone and Ling Mai remained.

Ling Mai looked from one to the other and paused before speaking to Vaughn. "If you have concerns, I will be available."

Then she departed.

Leaving only Vaughn and Stone.

Finger by finger, she unclenched her fists.

"You have a problem, princess?" he asked, his tone the same mocking, cynical one she'd heard so often over the past weeks.

Only then did she look at him. No way would she reveal the effort it took her to simply stand there, looking as calm and controlled as he did, not when her insides lay gutted, her dream ash in her throat. But to show any of the emotions tumbling through her meant defeat. And she wasn't about to give up.

"Just one little problem." She was surprised her voice didn't frost the room.

He arched a brow, but gave no response.

"You do that again, Stone, and you're a dead man."

"We talking about the kiss?"

"Forget the kiss. It meant nothing. We're talking about blindsiding me in front of my team."

"Your team?"

"You heard me, my team."

"We're supposed to be on the same team here." His voice deepened. "You forgetting that?"

"I'm forgetting nothing."

"Good, then remember this." His eyes heated as before, when only she could see them. He stepped closer, but she stood her ground, though every nerve ending screamed at her to flee. "You remember that I'm running this op. Not you. I'm senior member here. Not you. If I say jump, you jump. If I say retreat, you retreat."

"I don't do retreat."

"You will if I say so."

This time, she stepped forward, close enough so that she could smell the scent of his skin, see his breathing grow shallow.

Keep focused, she reminded herself. Their knee-jerk, physical responses and the tension they created didn't matter. Not with this man.

This was not personal; this was business.

"While we're setting things straight here, Stone, it's time you understand one thing."

"What's that?"

"I don't quit." Something turned molten in his gaze, but she kept talking. "I don't back down, run away or go crying to Daddy. No matter what you think. You can't make me. I won't let you."

"You sure about that?"

The thinly veiled threat hung there.

Vaughn had once seen two bulls in a field, preparing for battle, massive legs dug deep into the earth, nostrils flaring, shoulders hunched, neither willing to give an inch, both determined to win. She ached for the mindless animals then, for herself now.

"You have no idea what you're getting into." Stone broke the impasse, his words a whisper brushing across her raw emotions. "This is not a game."

"For me it never was."

If she gave this man an inch, he'd have her off the team and out of the program faster than...well, faster than he'd moved in for that kiss. The one she still tasted on her lips.

He was the one who backed away first.

That surprised her, though she didn't doubt for a moment that it wasn't a retreat but rather a tactical move, a regrouping. Stone hadn't given up. And neither would she.

"Be ready." He turned on his heel.

"I always am."

Too bad he didn't hear her as he'd already left.

So now where was she? Her first mission, her first chance to make a difference, to matter, and she was using her past as a calling card while she acted like Stone's wife.

Some days went to hell faster than others.

Well, she'd told him she wasn't a quitter, nor a whiner. He'd made his point, a very public point that he could manipulate her physical responses at the drop of a hat.

Score one for the rock man.

Now it was her turn. She had her own point to make. If Stone could make her peers think there was chemistry between the two of them, then Vaughn could be just as consummate an actress. And more so.

And if Ling Mai thought Vaughn was nothing more than a pawn, playing at being an operative, the older woman was in for a huge surprise.

Vaughn would do whatever it took to prove both Ling Mai and Stone wrong. With a sigh welling from her gut, Vaughn straightened her shoulders.

Twelve hours. She had twelve hours to get her mind where it needed to be to see this farce through. Not farce—mission—and the sham of a marriage along with it. And she'd do it.

She hadn't made it this far to quit now.

Chapter 8

Vaughn had to give Ling Mai credit—the woman created a huge splash of a public wedding. With paparazzi hanging out on every corner to catch a glimpse of the rich and famous, there could be no better locale to stage an eye-catching spectacle sure to be buzzed across every tabloid before sundown than the Hamptons, playground to the rich, the nouveaux riches and the famous for generations.

She and Stone had only returned from the beachside ceremony less than an hour ago and now they were sitting in a Manhattan sidewalk café, glancing at the first papers hot off the press.

The paparazzi had done their job well. Front page. Large bold type.

Ex-Ambassador's Daughter Marries Man Of Mystery.

CIA-Head Daughter Wed To Man With Dubious Past.

Socialite Says I Do In Private Affair—Family Absent.

Vaughn's private hope—that a hotshot celebrity breaking up with hubby number whatever would push all other news to a back page—was not realized. In fact, judging by the scope and sheer number of headlines, Vaughn suspected Ling Mai had asked everyone who could string a sentence together to write a juicy tidbit about the surprise wedding.

So much for being invisible. And to think she'd wanted to become an agent to quietly go about making a difference.

What a joke. Too bad she couldn't laugh at the absurdity of it all. Even now, sitting here with the warm afternoon sun spilling over the umbrella-shaded table, Vaughn battled the cold dread tightening her stomach.

The click of a Nikon not far away made her cringe and Stone frown. He grumbled beneath his breath. "At least in India we won't be front-page gossip."

As if paparazzi only hung out in New York. They should be so lucky. No point in stating the obvious, or at least the obvious to someone from her background.

Speaking of which, what was her family going to say?

That was the million-dollar question roping her stomach into Gordian knots, while even now a smile remained plastered on her face, her mimosa untouched.

In spite of the last-minute notice, Vaughn had managed to snag a vintage Prada oyster-and-sage floor-length gown to wear with a pair of antique diamond and jade earrings from her aunt Francine. Once news of the nuptials got out, no doubt it'd be the last Vaughn heard from anyone in her family. Tacky, tasteless and inappropriate would be the headlines, according to Vaughn's mother.

And Vaughn couldn't blame her. Not when her mother could not be told the truth behind the wedding-with-a-total-stranger scenario.

"You look worried." It was Stone across from her, startling Vaughn out of her musings.

"Not at all." She grabbed her tall glass and held it as if it were the last lifeline thrown from the *Titanic*. "Not worried." She smoothed a strand of hair back into her loose chignon, aware that her hand trembled slightly. "Just surprised that we need to go to these lengths. Couldn't a fake marriage certificate have worked just as well?"

"Not for the daughter of a former ambassador and the current CIA director. Your Russian friend would wonder why there had been no notice of your wedding in the press and would have suspected something was not as it should be."

He was right, as usual, but that didn't make Vaughn any less apprehensive. Becoming an undercover operative was one thing; getting married, even if it wasn't for real, was another. Especially when the guy she was getting hitched to was M. T. Stone, looking calm, controlled and sexy as hell as he lounged in the wire chair across from her.

And getting married in a very, very public glare put her front and center back into the world she'd been trying so hard to leave behind.

Another camera clicked. Her smile remained cemented in place.

"There is still time to turn back." Stone's words whispered against her while the blare of New York cabs and street voices bustled past.

"No." Vaughn shook her head, unsure of so much except this: she was committed to her new life, to her new calling, and if marrying M. T. Stone was the price she paid, then she'd pay it, eyes wide open. "I'm fine with this."

"Relax." Stone slid one hand along the table, covering hers with his. It took every ounce of her willpower not to jump, for more than one reason. But any lingering paparazzi, and there were a few, would have a field day with the intimacy. She could already hear the cameras shifting into hyperdrive. "I'm not the enemy here."

Yeah, right, like she was about to believe that statement for even a heartbeat.

If Stone guessed her thoughts, he ignored them. He scooted his chair toward her in a gesture that, coming from another, might have been protective, shielding her from the press and stares of the other diners closest to them.

"My first mission I shook like a rabbit caught in headlights," he said, sipping from his own glass of champagne, his gaze locked with hers over the rim.

What was he up to now? Another test?

"You being nice, Stone?" She was sure only he could hear her words. "Because if you are, don't bother. I don't need it."

"You sure?"

"I'm not scared and I'm not backing down." She raised her chin a notch.

"Never expected you to." He actually gave her a grin, a sexy, lopsided grin scrambling a few nerve endings. No doubt because she had sipped more champagne and orange juice than she should have on an empty stomach. One sip being too many with that kind of smile.

"What are you up to, Stone?" Men with potent smiles should have warning labels tattooed on them.

He raised one hand, lightly brushing the pad of his thumb ever so gently against her cheekbone, tucking a strand of hair behind her ear. "Have I told you that you look beautiful today?"

Had she heard him right, or had he lost it? Or had she stepped into the rabbit's hole for wanting to believe his words, the dark depths of his eyes?

Fortunately her cell phone rang, saving her from some totally inappropriate response.

She cleared her throat before answering, "Hello?"

"Vaughn." Her father's voice slapped against her. Everything in the restaurant and the street nearby receded, even Stone, sitting so close his sleeve brushed her bare arm.

"Hello, Father."

Maybe it was her imagination, but Stone stiffened at

her side and moved closer. Or maybe it was only herself, bracing for what would come next.

"Tell me it isn't true."

"You'll need to be more specific—"

"Enough, Vaughn. This wedding. I just heard, through official channels."

"Oh, that." She glanced at Stone, but didn't really see him, only the expanse of his white shirt against a broad chest. "Yes, as a matter of fact, it is true."

"Of all the—"

"Shall I give your congratulations to Stone, Father? He's sitting right here."

No point in only one of them being mauled to death, but of course her father wouldn't take the bait.

"What am I going to tell your mother?"

Vaughn sucked in a lungful of New York air. "I'll explain everything to Mother later. When I can."

"That's not good enough and you know it."

Salt poured into a wound.

Of all the people on the face of the planet, Vaughn expected a modicum of understanding from her father. But why should she have expected it now, when he had never understood her needs before? Still, her heart squeezed.

"Father." She used her most level voice, the one her mother had taught her in many a social drawing room. "This is not the best time to discuss this."

Not with an unsecured cell line and Stone breathing down her neck, no doubt waiting for any chink in her control.

"I am coming up there." Her father's voice told her it was not negotiable.

"I won't be here."

"What!"

"I'm leaving tomorrow. On my honeymoon."

Listen to me, Dad. Listen to what I can't say. You know what I'm doing, who I'm now working for. Please understand.

"I'm putting an end to this. Immediately." He hung up before she could reply.

She turned to Stone, every motion awkward and stiff. "You'd better tell Ling Mai to expect a call. Or worse."

"The old man not happy with his new son-in-law?"

Was he making a joke? At a time like this, when she was crumbling by the second? No wonder he confused her. But hadn't he also been the one who'd taught the recruits to use whatever weapon was at hand?

Vaughn took another breath, this one to slow her pulse and order her thoughts. "My father could cause problems."

There. She'd handed Stone a weapon if he chose to use it. What better excuse to pull a new operative than the fact that her very presence in an operation could create a backlash against the Agency.

"Ling Mai can handle herself." He acted as if they were discussing a speed bump instead of a train wreck.

"But—"

"We have enough to deal with, Monroe. Don't invite trouble."

Oh, that was choice, spoken by Mega Trouble Stone,

telling her to calm down. She didn't know if she wanted to thank him or sling her mimosa at him. And wouldn't that scene make a good photo op for the press.

He grinned again, as if understanding her every thought, an intimate, conspiratorial grin that had her realizing how very dangerous this man was to her, as an enemy, or as a friend.

"You never told me how you met this Russian," he said, throwing her for another loop.

"You never asked."

"I'm asking now."

"Fine." What could it hurt? "I was at a festival in Denmark one October a few years back."

"The Sex Festival in Copenhagen?"

Of course Stone would know about that particular festival. "Matter of fact, it was."

"I hear that can get pretty rowdy."

Understatement. She shrugged. "I guess you could say that."

"And you met Golumokoff there? Interesting?"

"It wasn't like that." Exactly. "I met him in a nightclub, with a whole group of people."

"And?"

"And, after the club closed, this group was heading out to another club." She paused.

"What happened?"

Only because his voice no longer sounded accusing could she continue. "And one of the guys didn't want to take no for an answer. So I headed back to my hotel. Alone."

He said nothing, so she plowed forward, rubbing the condensation on the glass back and forth. "Except this creep decided to follow me. I thought it'd be fine. The hotel wasn't far, it was in the middle of Copenhagen. Lots of people around."

"But?"

"But he caught me by surprise and decided to get rough."

The rough shove to the pavement. A hand squeezing her throat. The world graying.

"Was the guy Golumokoff?"

"No. Blade noticed the guy following me and tagged along behind him." She leaned closer to Stone so he would understand. "If it wasn't for Blade, I doubt I'd be here."

"So you feel you owe him."

"I *do* owe him."

He looked as if he were about to say something more but Jayleen, Alex and Mandy joined them. Instead, he leaned forward and whispered, "Plane leaves for India in a few hours. Don't be late."

Then he rose and strode away, in that arrogant, cocky walk of his that said he'd had the last word.

"You're looking pretty intense." Alex slid into a chair at her side. "What are you thinking?"

"Of all the ways one could kill Stone."

Alex gulped back a laugh. "If the man I just married had a butt that cute in tight pants, it wouldn't be murder I had on *my* mind."

"The marriage is a fake," Vaughn reminded her.

"Yeah." Alex shrugged. "But the honeymoon doesn't have to be."

"So do not go there."

"But—"

"I think Vaughn has a few more issues to worry about." Jayleen's voice overrode Alex's, her face serious.

Great. One more battle in a day already chock-full of them.

"You have something to say?" Vaughn asked. "If so, spit it out."

"Fine." The woman slapped a card down on the table in front of Vaughn.

Vaughn said nothing, even as Alex sucked in her breath.

"That doesn't look so good," Alex said.

Even a ninny would recognize this card. The one with a grinning skeleton staring from the center of a field of fiery flowers.

"If this is supposed to be a joke, Jayleen, it's not funny."

Vaughn moved to stand, but Jayleen's hand to her wrist halted her.

"It's not what it looks like," she said.

Alex nudged Mandy. "Hey, we've got to get going. See you all at the plane." She cast an anxious glance at Vaughn before adding, "Don't worry, we're here to back you."

Then she and the new girl disappeared. Smart women.

"You've got something to say, Jayleen, say it. But this crap about death cards is not appreciated."

"The card is about profound change, which, if resisted, may be painful."

"Nice."

"I mean it. The cards are only meant to give fair warning. Old patterns must be destroyed, released in order to make room for the new."

"Great. I'll remember that, now if you don't mind—"

"Look, Vaughn, there ain't a lot of love lost between us and we both know it."

"Your point?"

"My point is, you're about to face your greatest fears, and they can do one of two things. Make you stronger…"

"Or?"

"Or destroy you."

Chapter 9

India—bleating animals wandering the streets, car horns blaring, dust mingling with masses of people, wrapping one in a blanket both suffocating and irritating. The monsoons had not yet broken the dry heat; an air of expectancy choked human and animal alike.

Even the Hotel Taj was not immune, though it was one of the nicest of the older hotels in Simla's stately mall area, a haven of postcolonial British-looking homes and shops. Another contrast in a country of contrasts. Vaughn wondered how Ling Mai had arranged for rooms, since they were usually booked for months ahead of time as city dwellers and travelers headed north to find relief until the rains arrived.

Inside the Taj's marble hallways, one could forget, for a few moments, the echo of humanity on the other side of its intricately carved doors. The odors of jasmine planted around the open verandah, the dark aroma of teak furniture and sweat—the bellboys, hotel help and her own travel-creased wear—smacked Vaughn in the face.

She'd actually missed this part of the world.

Everyone looked rumpled and on edge, typical right before the dry season ended and the blessed wet arrived. More suicides and murders occurred at this time of year than any other as nerves stretched to the breaking point, testing the patience of even the most determined of Hindu saints.

And then there was Stone.

Vaughn stood away from the reception desk, her whole attention fixed on him, looking cool and controlled as usual, registering the two of them into the hotel as Mr. and Mrs. Stone. He looked like a world traveler, in khaki pants and a lightweight Armani jacket that on someone else would have been wrinkled. It made him even more eye-catching—sexy, urbane James Bond in action.

They'd traveled straight through from New York, awake twenty-three hours and counting. Right now, all Vaughn wanted was a soft bed and blessed oblivion. Or even a few minutes away from Stone's hawklike gaze. The man missed nothing, which might have reassured her if it were someone else, but with him it was like waiting for a chopping blade to strike.

But she wasn't here to sleep, nor to wait for Stone to act; she was quite capable of acting herself.

With a small wave, she signaled to a bellhop with al-mond-shaped eyes and thick, dark eyelashes to die for.

"Yes, Missy?" he asked, his voice wavering between adolescent and adult.

She fingered a handful of five rupee coins as she leaned close. "Is there a Mister Golumokoff in the hotel?" At the boy's puzzled expression, she tried again. "A Russian, so tall." She held her hand a good foot above her own head. "Big shoulders. Yellow hair. Big men always near him."

"Oh, yes, Missy. Man is here."

She squeezed a little more information from the boy before she slipped the coins into his hands.

Right then, her cell phone buzzed. She looked at the incoming number and debated answering, but obliga-tion won out.

"Hello, Mother."

"Vaughn? Vaughn, is that you?"

You tell me, you're the one calling. Vaughn sighed. *Manners, Vaughn. Mind your manners.* She forced a smile on her face, if not her tone. "Yes, Mother, it's me."

"Tell me you didn't. You couldn't. Not like this. Not after all—"

"Mother, the connection is bad." Vaughn scraped her nails across the speaker.

"You just couldn't," her mother continued, a female Sherman tank on the roll. "Chrissie told me to expect something like this."

What were sisters for?

"But I never believed that—"

Vaughn counted to seven, knowing by ten either the *health* card or the *friends* card would be brought to bear.

"I can't imagine how we'll tell our friends."

So health would be saved for a bigger issue.

"Mother, Mother, can you hear me?" The quickest way to stop her mother was to use her own trump cards. "Mother, ask Father."

"—down at the club. What?"

"You heard me, ask Father."

"About what?"

Vaughn glanced up as Stone started to approach. "Father knows what's happening."

"But he never—"

"Ciao, Mother. Love to Grams. Hugs to Chrissie." Who, no doubt, was standing in the background gloating over screwup Vaughn earning another black mark.

"But, Vaughn, you can't."

"Talk to Father. Bye." She clicked her phone shut with enough force to snap the rhinestone-studded clamshell in two.

"Problem?" Stone asked, returning to her side.

"Of course not."

"Vaughn?" He simply stood there looking at her with those dark eyes carefully blanked, close enough to telegraph intimacy should anyone look. Heavy-lidded. Sexy. Dangerous. And posing as her lover.

The role, dummy, she reminded herself. He's playing the role. As should she.

"Sorry, jet lag." She had to remember she was in her

territory now. It'd been a few years since she'd visited India, but it was more familiar to her than the setup at the headquarters in Maryland had been. Her turf, her terms.

If she could only focus on it. And forget Mother. And Father. And her old debt to Blade. The list was getting longer by the minute.

The multiple clicks of cameras not far away jolted her back to reality. Paparazzi.

"So much for being invisible," Stone murmured close to her side. "Remind me to wring Ling Mai's neck."

"Gladly."

Instead of letting him brush past the trio of photographers she snagged his arm and turned her body sideways against him. An intimate pose that said more than any words ever could.

"What the—" Stone growled.

"My world, darling." She smiled brightly, hoping her face didn't crack. "Feed the vultures scraps and they'll go away. Remain elusive and you become a bigger target."

He glanced at her and lowered his voice. "You do know what the word *covert* means, don't you?"

She bussed him on the cheek and smiled brighter, her nails biting into his arm as she whispered, "Don't snap at me, darling. I didn't set up this fiasco."

He remained quiet. The way a volcano remained quiet, calm on the surface, ready to blow at any time.

By the time the paparazzi departed and they reached their spacious room, she wondered if she was already in way over her head. The mission had barely begun.

Stone groaned aloud as two bellhops brought in her luggage. He waited until they left before saying, "Ever hear of the term *traveling light?*"

"Not in my world, darling." She breezed past him. "This is a honeymoon. If I showed up with one suitcase less than this—" she waved a hand toward the leather Louis Vuittons "—our cover would be blown before we started. Trust me on this."

To her surprise, he did. At least that was what she took his shrug to mean before he became the skilled operative, checking for listening devices, scouting out escape routes, memorizing the terrain.

She stood in the middle of the room and looked at the bed. The only bed, smaller than the California King back in her apartment.

"Got a problem?" he asked, not even looking at her.

A hard slap would have stung less.

"No problem." She cleared a desert-dry throat. "What's next on the agenda?"

There. She could do this. Cool. Controlled. Professional.

His smile telegraphed that he saw right through her.

"Depends on you." He walked to the balcony with its open louvered wooden doors, though no breeze wafted through them. "If you need downtime, take it. It's been a long day."

Understanding from him or another test? She figured the latter.

He continued, "On the other hand, if you're ready to operate, best place to run into your boyfriend would probably be the verandah. Several chairs are occupied."

She figured right; it was a test.

"For the record, Blade was never my boyfriend." Not that the opportunity hadn't been there, but no need to discuss that with Stone. She crossed to stand beside him, gazing out across the grassy courtyard below, the Himalayas large smudges on the horizon. "And Blade would never be caught in a lounge chair in the middle of the day."

One dark eyebrow arched as he shrugged. "You know him better than I."

"There." She pointed to a gazebo set in a grove of banyan trees, their trunks offering as much shade as their leaves. "If he's around at all today, he'll be there."

"Because?"

"Private. Removed. With the best view of all the traffic coming in and out of the hotel. Besides, I checked with the bellboy. Blade has been spending his afternoons there, early evenings in the private lounge."

He gave her another smile. "Well done." He glanced away. "So he's a strategist."

"He's a survivor." *A lot like you,* she wanted to add, then wondered where the thought came from. "Have you checked in with Alex or Jayleen's team?"

"Later tonight. We can update them on contact with Golumokoff."

We? It sounded strange. Must be the heat and travel getting to her.

She glanced at her watch. "Afternoon tea will be over soon, cocktails not for another hour. That's when we should make our move."

He nodded. "Your call."

So maybe they'd made progress, until he added, "On this."

Players in a game within another game, a world she recognized, if under a different guise.

She headed toward the bathroom and a cool shower, hoping it would help get her thoughts clear and focused on where they needed to be—the mission.

Stone was waiting for her when she came through the hotel's wide set of double doors and out into the heavy evening heat. Waiting and watching. As was she.

She looked different than the sweat-suited recruit he'd trained over the last several weeks. She'd chosen a silky chiffon polka-dot dress by Etro that had hung in her own closet, its folds whispering around her, soft and feminine, as was the large brimmed hat she wore. Her hair was swept up off the nape of her neck, a few wisps escaping. She floated more than moved and was aware that more than one male eye appreciated her as she crossed from the paved verandah to the grassy verge.

But not Stone. He barely moved or gave anything away. Except for the narrowing of his eyes. He'd be appalled to have betrayed even that much, but she'd been looking for it.

So M.T. could mean Maybe Tempted.

Good. She wasn't alone in this dangerous physical

chemistry buzzing between the two of them; no matter how smugly superior he wanted to act, rock man had a chink.

She wafted up to him in a cloud of perfume, charm and silk. The man wasn't going to know what hit him.

"You're late." His gaze narrowed.

So maybe she'd have to work a little harder. Or clobber him.

But she was saved from finding out which when a very dark, huskily accented voice washed over her.

"Vaughn, is that not you?"

She watched Stone's gaze slip past her shoulder and narrow before she turned.

"Blade? I don't believe it." She stepped into his open embrace as if it'd been days, not years, since she'd seen him, surprised at the sense of connection. So maybe she'd played up the "just friends" part of their relationship a little more than she should have, especially in light of how happy he looked to see her.

The years had been kind to him, giving his patrician face more interesting angles, his charming smile more depth. Only his eyes hadn't changed. They were a deep sea gray that changed with his moods, shifted from gunmetal determined to the silver-pearl color of an ocean's sunset. Now they were steel bright, and appraising.

"It has been far, far too long. I never see you anymore. And you have changed. Grown up into a beautiful woman, no longer a tempting child." He held her longer and closer than necessary for old friends, but she didn't protest. "You have been too busy for your old comrade."

Now there was an interesting Russian word, spanning the ambiguity of their earlier relationship. More than friends, less than lovers. What could time have wrought between them, if she had not stepped away?

Self-preservation or wariness? She never could pin down her hesitation to commit one way or another then; the uncertainty was still present now.

Belatedly she recalled her role and stepped back.

"Our paths never cross." She gave a light shrug. "I think you are the one who is too busy. Nanette, or maybe it was Monica, said you are now a bourgeois businessman, always making money, too busy to play."

Her words were meant to focus him on his past and not hers.

The barb hit home. He released her, held her at arm's length; his voice was still jovial, his eyes less so. "Never too busy for a beautiful woman. Before you were a girl, a ripening peach, but now—" He spread his arms wide. "But now you are so much more."

It was flowery, opulent and overstated, but after dealing with Stone for the last three months, it sounded darn good.

She gave Blade a warm smile. The man might be a suspected criminal with a ruthless reputation, but he did know how to treat a woman when he chose to. Maybe Stone could learn a few lessons.

"I have missed you." She offered him a genuine smile. "And you have not changed at all."

A deep cough interrupted Blade's response and

Vaughn watched the Russian acknowledge Stone for the first time.

"And this is?" he asked, his accent thickening, the two bodyguards flanking him shifting closer.

"I'm so sorry," she soothed, turning to include Stone in the conversation. "Blade, I would like you to meet M.T."

"M.T.?" Blade repeated.

Stone stepped forward, extending a hand. The move appeared friendly, as long as you didn't look at the set of his face.

"Marcos. Marcos T. Stone. Vaughn's husband."

Chapter 10

"Your husband, he is not what I would have expected for you." Blade brushed an invisible piece of lint from his dinner jacket. They stood together in the very small, very crowded bar of the Taj lounge; Blade was throwing a party for a few of his business associates and friends, none of whom Vaughn recognized. Which wasn't a surprise, considering India was off the map for many in their former crowd, and the passage of years had also brought changes.

Vaughn took it as a good sign when Blade had invited them.

Marcos? Could that be his real name? Somehow it fit him—ruthless, exotic and dark. Unfortunately, it rolled through her thoughts a little too easily.

She caught a commotion near the open doorway leading from the main hotel to the lounge and glanced in that direction. Kelly stood there, looking like the quintessential tourist, rumpled, wide-eyed and in culture shock.

"Oh." The blonde raised one hand to her mouth, brushing two obvious cameras slung across her chest. Vaughn was aware Kelly carried two others, discretely hidden and even now snapping photos. "Am I interrupting something?"

One of Blade's security guards stepped to Kelly's side, quickly and efficiently steering her away from the group. Another group of photographers raised cameras high, snapping a few shots of Vaughn without Stone at her side. She could imagine the headlines already. *Honeymoon Over, What Went Wrong? Trouble In Paradise? Wed In Haste, Regret In...*

"Vaughn, you are not listening." Blade's accent deepened, a sign of annoyance. He glanced at the doorway, a frown marring his expression. "You wish me to remove them?"

"No." She shook herself, sure Kelly would be all right and hoping the photographers would not bother Blade as she smiled at him. "Forgive me. It has been a long day and we only arrived this afternoon. What were you saying?"

"I spoke of your husband. He is not, how you say, your type?"

"Oh." Blade's English diction was better than her own, but he slipped into the cadence of his mother country when it suited him. Like now. He was on a fishing expedition, and she wasn't surprised. "I think Stone suits me fine."

"He watches you all the time. He is very dark, this man."

She followed Blade's gaze as it rested on Stone, standing slightly apart from those nearest him, watching the crowd but not part of it.

"Dark in what way?" Vaughn took a sip of her tepid drink and wished for a breath of cooler night air from the open verandah doors.

"What does he do for a living? Does he work with your father?"

So they were going to play fifty questions. Fine. She'd been drilled on this. Stone's deep cover was well in place.

"Don't be silly, Blade, you know better than most the last man I'd be with would resemble dear old Dad." Funny, that had once been the truth, and still was as far as Blade needed to know. A good place to start; now for the rest. "I don't know much about Stone's business beyond the fact it keeps him very busy, traveling widely, and makes him filthy rich. Imports and exports, he says."

She flirted with Blade over the rim of her glass, knowing his attention had picked up with the ubiquitous term *import and export.* Every smuggler, operator and security bureau in the world used the same cover story. Their own private shorthand.

"I see." Blade nodded to a man near the front entrance, who nodded back and disappeared. "And you married him because?"

"It seemed like a good idea at the time." Vaughn

kept her voice light and mocking, a skill learned young in her circle of world friends, many too wealthy and too bored to know how similar they all sounded.

"I read about the event." Blade took a sip of his own drink but his gaze remained heavy on hers. "*Herald Tribune,* I believe, though they do not make note of many such events."

So Ling Mai was correct—press coverage did matter. Score one for the director. Vaughn simply smiled, letting Blade continue.

"You are happy?" Blade asked, his tone touching her with the concern rimming it.

"Stone has his moments." She glanced toward the man under discussion. "He makes a nice change from those in the old group who are happy to settle down to nappies, nannies and normalcy."

"Ah, you still seek the excitement, the thrill, do you not?"

She shrugged, leaving him to interpret it any way he wanted. His gaze shifted and a chill slid across her exposed shoulders, one that had nothing to do with the outside temperature.

Stone had materialized at her side.

"You are enjoying my friends?" Blade spoke to him, playing the role of congenial host well.

"You have an interesting crowd of acquaintances." Stone slid one hand across Vaughn's lower back and she flinched. The man really should warn her. Thankfully Blade's attention was on Stone, one predator sizing up another.

Stone continued, "Vaughn did not mention your business."

"They are many." Blade waved one hand. On a lesser man the gesture would have been very feminine; on the Russian it was grand and dismissive. "Many dealing with imports and exports."

"Is that so."

Stalemate.

Vaughn ratcheted up her smile, speaking to Stone though not looking at him. "Blade knows the most fascinating people and used to throw the best parties."

"You flatter me, my dear." Blade reached for her hand and raised it to his lips, holding it there a heartbeat too long.

He really was impossible, and maybe their intel about him was wrong. Always a possibility.

Stone pressed closer to her, firmly lowering her arm with his hand as the air reversed in her lungs. "Flattery is only one of *my* wife's charms."

The hostility was unmistakable. Was the man trying to get both of them killed?

Blade's eyes slitted to flat lines as his face tightened. The conversation around them stilled, then stuttered to silence as others caught the scent of battle.

"M.T., learn your manners." She wished her voice sounded less thin as she turned to Blade. "You'll have to forgive him. M.T. was not raised in a cosmopolitan society."

"Is that so?"

Stone did not answer, but she didn't have to glance

at his face to guess his expression. She'd seen it
enough times over the last weeks to have it branded
on her memory. Cynical. Mocking. Daring. Goad
your enemy without words, a neat trick if one got
away with it.

No one moved until Blade straightened and smiled,
a shark's dinner grin.

"It is only right that a man is possessive about his
woman." He turned toward Vaughn. "If you were mine,
I would be so, too."

And here she'd thought they were in the twenty-
first century.

She kept her own stiff smile in place, too aware of
Stone's touch branding her arm and her back. "You are
very kind."

"Not at all, my dear." Blade's look deepened and that
temperature drop she'd been hoping for earlier finally
materialized, but it had nothing to do with a change in
the weather outside. "In fact, I was just about to ask you
and your husband here to be my guests over the next
few days. At a very private party not far away."

"Oh, that would be—"

"We'll let you know." Stone tightened his grip on her
arm, sloshing her drink as he wheeled her around.
"Come along, darling." He spoke to Vaughn, the endear-
ment as mocking as his *princess*. "It's late and we've
had a long day."

She barely had time to nod to Blade, who watched
them until they disappeared into the hallway.

A very crowded hallway, as was the elevator.

It wasn't until they reached their room that she could demand, "Do you want to tell me what the—"

Stone was there, his hand across her mouth, his gaze burning her as he leaned close, close enough for her to hear his heartbeat as he whispered in her ear. "Listening devices."

Damn.

He kept his tone that of a frustrated spouse as he stepped back, his gaze still locked with hers. "You're angry, Vaughn. I suggest you step out on the verandah to cool down."

His look said, *Don't blow this any more than you already have.*

Echoes of childhood chastisement rang in her memory.

Don't be silly, Vaughn.

You should have known better, Vaughn.

Vaughn, when will you ever learn to behave properly?

She walked, knees locked to the verandah, watching him scout the room before joining her, his voice still in his role as he said, "Let's take a walk. It might be cooler downstairs on the lawn."

She followed him silently, bracing herself to accept any lecture he had to give, none of which could compete with the lectures she was already giving herself.

She was supposed to be a pro. To listen to his cues and play along. Less than a day into the mission and she was already running around like a blind and deaf idiot.

What if she'd said more when they'd reached the room? Hadn't she noticed the man Blade had nodded to earlier? Of course he'd been sent as an advance scout to reconnoiter her and Stone's room. She should have realized that.

"We should be safe here." Stone's voice was as dark and deep as the shadows bracketing the gazebo near the banyan tree.

Before he could say more, she shook her head, her eyes adjusting to the shadows. "I blew it back there. I'm sorry."

"For which part?"

How like the man not to let her off easy, though his tone held no heat.

"I should have realized the room had been bugged. Did you find any?"

"Three. Light socket, lamp and headboard. My take is your boyfriend is a bit of a voyeur."

That didn't surprise her. What did was the hard slap of her emotions as they hit bottom. One day in and she'd yo-yoed from high to low and everywhere in between. If she and Stone had been who they said they were, the thought of another listening to their every word, their most private actions, revolted her.

Stone's hand brushed across her arm.

She jumped.

"You've got to watch that." He stepped away to lean against the gazebo rail, facing her. His expression danced in and out of focus in alternating shadow and light. "Most new wives don't flinch when their husbands touch them."

"Good point." As if it was going to make any difference. She wrapped her arms around herself, not chilled so much as disillusioned. Had she done anything right so far? Not that she expected Stone to acknowledge it, but it might have been nice. She moved closer so that her voice wouldn't carry. "I don't understand."

"What?"

"I thought we were here to get information from Blade. Wouldn't it be just as well to get invited to Brighton Hall and find out exactly what's going on?"

"Too dangerous. Our mission is to find the intel here then back off. The auction is a last resort."

How could she have forgotten so soon? An invite to Brighton Hall was only if she failed to get the information they needed here. On the other hand, if they had the opportunity, didn't it make sense to go where the action was? Only at Brighton Hall would they access not only intel on the item or items being auctioned, but all the players, as well.

But going to Brighton Hall would also mean that Ling Mai, and more importantly Stone, thought she could act as a full-fledged operative.

"How am I supposed to extract any intel if you're cutting me off before I can probe?" She sighed out of weariness and frustration before nodding over her shoulder. "By asking us to join him, Blade was opening up—"

"The man's a pro. He offers bait and we jump too soon, he'll suspect something is off. He might accept it from you, but not from me."

Great, another reminder of how incompetent she was.

"So we say no and hope he'll offer again?"

"He will."

"How can you be so sure?"

"He's a man and he wants you. You can see it in the way he looks at you."

The words sounded husky, though that could have been just her imagination. Blade's phrase came back to her—he watches you. Truth in either statement? Or wired hormones getting in the way?

She shook it off. "I don't think he wants me as much as to score one on you."

"Same thing." He stepped away from the rail until barely a hand's length separated them, that and the warm darkness of the night. "We'll use either. Both. By this time tomorrow, we'll have our intel."

"Or an invite to the auction." She didn't want to examine too closely why it was suddenly hard to breathe and speak at the same time.

He was staking a lot on a few moments' worth of conversation, but then again Stone was the pro, the one who'd kept his head and his role intact since they'd arrived. Maybe it was time to start giving him the benefit of the doubt.

Without a word, his hand came around her, pulling her closer. She looked up, noting the angle of his face in the half light, remembering paintings in the Louvre and Uffizi of demon lovers who seduced mortal maidens. Naive mortal maidens.

"What?" She whispered the single word as he looked at her intensely.

"Slap me."

"But—"

"Slap me hard." His arm tightened around her, his tone deepening and increasing in volume. "If you think you're going back—"

She did as she was ordered. Summoning all the frustration, all the humiliation of the last forty-eight hours, she used the flat of her hand against his cheek with a force that snapped his head back.

Only then did she hear shoes hitting the wooden steps of the gazebo.

"I am not interrupting a lovers' misunderstanding?" Blade's pronunciation now showed his Etonian English training, a smug assuredness deep in its tone.

"No." It probably helped matters that her own voice sounded short and breathless as she stepped away from Stone's arms, surprised that the night's temperatures had started to drop, hoping that alone explained the goose bumps trilling down her arms. "Not at all. M.T. understands me correctly now. Is that not so?"

The smile Stone flashed her was the devil's own grin, even with the dab of blood he brushed off his lower lip. "Absolutely, darling."

She should have hit him harder.

"Good night, Blade." She walked from the gazebo, her head higher than her confidence before she stopped. "And M.T., find your own place to sleep tonight."

That was why he'd staged the scene, set it up to explain to Blade what he would, and would not, be hearing in their hotel room. Yeah, Stone was a pro. But she was learning, too.

She just hoped she learned fast enough.

Chapter 11

Late in the afternoon two days later, Stone connected with Jayleen and Mandy. Vaughn stood next to him in the hot shade of the Jakhu Temple, a good forty-five minute walk from the Hotel Taj, far enough away from Blade and Blade's goons to be able to speak freely. Not that she expected Blade to be anywhere within sight of the temple built for Hanuman, the monkey god. Religious or historic sights were not his thing, even though the view here was spectacular. Not that one could enjoy the scenery in peace with the squeals and screams of the many monkeys inhabiting the courtyard and temple grounds.

She listened with half an ear as Stone used a head mike to connect with their backup team as there were no cell phone towers near enough to make easy calls, even if they believed that their calls would not be intercepted.

Only when he had finished the call did she turn his way.

"What news?" she asked.

"Alex is in place about two clicks from Brighton Hall. Camping."

"Isn't that a little rugged?"

"There are enough trekkers and alternative seekers at this time of year to explain her presence if she's found. Outside close range of the resort but near enough."

"And Jayleen and Mandy?"

"Here in town. They've set up a safe house not far from the Taj."

"That was quick."

He glanced at her, his look veiled. "Jayleen has her talents, one of them being an ability to make her way around a strange city."

Great. Now it sounded as if Vaughn was complaining about her teammate. Which she wasn't, not this time.

"I didn't mean—"

"Trust is important in a team."

Yeah, like he trusted her. No point in trying to explain, though; sometimes it was just better to swallow one's pride, even if you choked.

"Will they be in contact on a regular basis?" she asked.

"Not unless we call them in."

"And Kelly?"

"Has already transmitted a number of images to Ling Mai, who's processing them for recognition. So far, it looks like many are go-betweens, which means it's taking longer to make the connections between bidder and final buyer."

"So is that good news?" She tried to read his expression.

"No."

"Because?"

"Because the few that Ling Mai have identified have connections with several very dangerous, very nasty terrorist organizations."

Even a newbie op like her understood the implications of that statement, and they weren't good. But this was Blade. Her Blade, of the easy smiles and the warm friendship. She just couldn't—or didn't want to—think he was working hand in hand with the people Stone was describing. There must be some kind of explanation, but so far nothing came to mind.

"So it becomes even more imperative to find out what is being auctioned?" she asked.

"Exactly."

"Anything else?" She rubbed open palms along her khaki slacks.

Something was worrying him. Not that a rock man gave much away, but even his gaze was remote and removed, staring out toward the snow-capped Himalayas in the distance.

He tightened his jaw and turned to her. She snapped her shoulders to attention.

"Well?" she prompted when he hesitated.

"Jayleen passed along the news that Ling Mai has changed the mission in light of the players involved thus far." His tone sounded like pebbles dropping into deep, dark, bottomless water.

"In what way?"

"She wants us to get that invite to Brighton Hall."

If a heart could flatline while still beating, Vaughn's just did.

"And you agreed?" She waited for the pebble to hit bottom.

"I told her you weren't ready."

Nothing like anger to kick-start a reaction.

"Of all the—"

"Wait." He held up one hand, as if that was going to stop or even slow her down. "I also agreed. We don't have a lot of options in light of a new development."

Okay, she could let him know exactly what was lacking in his definition of *team*, or she could act like a professional, which she kept telling herself she was.

"What's the development?" Each word rolled like ground glass in her throat.

"It appears MI6 sent in two operatives last week to do exactly what we're doing."

That sounded like a good thing to her...or were they talking international rivalries here?

"And the problem is?" she prompted. "Can't we combine resources?"

He didn't glance her way, but she caught a shift in his mood before he said, "They found one of the agents this morning three blocks from the hotel. His throat slit."

Dead? The finality of Stone's words reverberated

through her. Who was the op? Man? Woman? Did he or she have a spouse, a lover, children?

Gone. Just like that. Wiped from the face of the earth.

"And the other agent?"

"Still missing."

Good news or bad? And what was Blade's involvement? Could the man who so gallantly kissed her hand only yesterday be so callous and heartless as to murder in cold blood? Or could there be another reason for an agent's death? Being an operative meant existing in a dark, violent world. Wasn't she learning that by the moment? Could the agent's death be due to something other than Blade's mysterious auction? Or was that her old life rearing its naive head? The one happy to look the other way and ignore the brutality of anything ugly, painful or messy.

Stone waited at her side, no doubt expecting her to waver and run.

"Blade isn't necessarily involved in the killing." Even as she uttered the words she sensed Stone's resistance.

"You still thinking you owe this guy?" he asked, shifting the conversation.

"I do."

"Not here you don't." The look Stone cast her told her to get real and grow up. Not necessarily in that order. "And if you can't grasp, or won't grasp that concept, the mission is over."

Fine. She'd asked to be an operative; nothing she did or didn't do was going to bring that British agent back. But what she did next might mean the agent hadn't died in vain.

"So what happens now?" she asked.

"If you have your head on straight, we exploit Golumokoff's vulnerability."

Leave it up to the man to throw her for a loop. She thought they'd be talking strategy, tactics, formulating a plan. What was he discussing?

"And that vulnerability is?"

"You." His appraising look made the thin mountain air nonexistent. He was pushing every button. Twice.

"You mind explaining that?"

"Your boyfriend is a man who doesn't like losing."

She kept her tone even, though not her temper. "I told you, he never was my boyfriend and he can't lose what he never had."

"That's your perspective." He glanced away. "Haven't you ever wanted something, but didn't get it? Then, for some reason, years later, it surfaces again? Another chance. Another opportunity. Only once again, it is out of your reach."

Yeah, she wanted to make a difference, but every turn she made complicated that goal. Clearing her throat, she focused on the topic at hand. "Because I'm supposedly married to you, or because I'm here means I'm now in reach?"

"A man like Blade wouldn't let a marriage vow stop him if he thought it meant getting what was denied to him before."

"And you know this because?"

"Because I wouldn't let it stop me." The dark, enigmatic look he shot her forced her to swallow.

Nothing personal. The man was talking in general-ities, not specifics. Think like a pro, not a woman.

"Fine." She let out a small whoosh of breath. "Let's say you're right. Somewhat."

His lips twitched into a reluctant grin, but she ignored it.

"So Blade wants to claim what he feels was denied him before, like he couldn't have any woman he wanted. Then, or now. The man is wealthy, intelligent, powerful and good-looking." There. She'd made her point, not that Stone wanted to hear her opinion. "But if this is about some macho male competitive thing—"

"It's not about competition, though there is some of that there. It's more about possession."

"You can't possess a person."

"You can possess what you feel another person has. Currently your Russian sees you belonging to me. Before, you belonged to your father. Either way, winning you over, by any means possible, sets him up as the stronger male. If I was out of the picture, you'd still be the daughter of the CIA director. A very enticing win for a man like Golumokoff."

It sounded like a textbook description of dangerous and unstable.

She cleared her throat and attributed the goose bumps on her skin to the temple shadows, nothing more. "So what happens next?"

"You, or more specifically I, turned down his first attempt to lure you the other night."

"Lure? You make me sound like some Gothic ninny."

"You're a woman. He's a man. Lure. Entice. Seduce. Use whatever term you want. Other women might fall for the points you mentioned—money, looks, power— but you wouldn't."

Deep, dangerous water, with eddies and whirlpools, and hidden monsters lurking everywhere.

She eased onto the shoals. "And you know this because?"

"Because you never fell for him the first time around."

"I told you, our relationship wasn't like that."

"No, you have a trigger that's different."

She should have slapped him harder the other night.

"And that trigger is?"

"Your boyfriend thinks it's excitement. He thinks you're a wind junkie—like him."

"A wind junkie?" She'd crewed and soloed enough sailboats to realize he was talking about those who sailed against the wind, craving the rush of air and speed and water—the surge of power when one pitted oneself against nature—the razor-edge experience.

He continued, "That's what the auctions are about for your friend. They're as much about skirting the law, possessing that which can't be possessed, and knowing at any time one could be caught."

He was right. Wrong about Blade and her, but right about the auctions.

"So what does this have to do with getting into the auction at Brighton Hall?"

"By saying no to the man, we put you just a little more outside his reach."

"And you think that's going to make me more attractive to him? If he can—what was the word you used? Lure?—if he can lure me to the auction, he'll have scored twice. Whetted my appetite and pissed you off at the same time."

"Exactly."

She found herself laughing. This wasn't high school. On the other hand, many of life's lessons were best learned in the heady emotional turmoil of those teenage years. Game playing. Risk avoidance. The cost of caring too much.

Her laugh died away. "So I'm now the bait, and no longer just the doorway to an introduction."

He didn't answer right away, not until she let her gaze lock with his; she wished she hadn't. One could not hide from those dark eyes.

"What?" she asked, when the waiting and the scream of monkeys jangled already twitching nerves.

"None of this is personal."

Oh, that was priceless. She was the one being examined and dissected like a lab animal, and he had the gall to say it wasn't personal.

"It might not be to you. This is just another job to you." Her breath hitched, but she continued, "An assignment I know you didn't want, but it has nothing to do with your past life. No skeletons in the closet for M. T. Stone. No warts, no stupid mistakes you made that you wish you could undo, no—"

He stopped her the same way he had the other night, except instead of his whole hand covering her mouth he simply laid two fingers across her lips. Very gently. Very firmly. Very effectively.

Damn him anyway. How dare he make her heart skip a beat and her hands curl into useless fists.

He waited, using that rocklike patience of his, until she stilled her pesky emotions and nodded. Only then did he let his fingers slide away.

"We all have shadows in our closets." He spoke with the tang of remorse. "The key to staying alive in this job is to make sure those past mistakes don't come back to bite you."

Easy for him to say.

He smiled, though there was little humor in it. "A wise man once said an expert is only a man who's made every mistake once."

"Great. I'm well on my way." She meant the remark to be light; instead it sounded strained.

He shrugged. "Yeah. You are."

A compliment? From Stone? Not in a million years.

He turned to head back to the path toward town when she stopped him by laying a hand on his arm.

"What happens now?" she asked, bracing herself for his answer.

"We use the situation to our advantage."

"You mean use what you think is Blade's attraction to me as the bait to get us into the auction."

"Isn't that what I said?"

She bit her lower lip before continuing; she had to make clear to him where she was coming from. "You're wrong, you know."

"About?"

"About my being a wind junkie. That's not my trigger."

"I said that's what Golumokoff thinks. Not me." He turned to leave again, but paused. "One more thing."

"Yes?"

"Your father is putting pressure on Ling Mai. He wants you out of this op as much as I do. It'd behoove you to not screw up."

He strode away, while she remained, simmering with anger.

He was very good at that. Dropping bombs and walking away. On the other hand, it looked like they were making progress. He'd called Blade by his name, not *boyfriend*.

"You're reaching for reassurances," she whispered to a monkey staring at her from a stone wall three feet away.

The only answer she received was a solemn stare.

Chapter 12

She'd agreed to meet Stone on the terrace later that evening. The night sky was filled with stars, and lighted paper lanterns dotted the shadows.

Tonight she was not planning on being invisible. Tonight Vaughn was on her own mission—to prove to herself she had what it took to be a field agent, regardless of what anyone else thought. And to do that she needed to get the information from Blade about the item or items to be auctioned, or receive an invite to the auction. And she'd be doing it her way.

To accomplish less would mean the end of what she'd barely started. With her father pulling strings and putting pressure on Ling Mai to remove Vaughn from the team, time was of the essence. If Vaughn could not find out what was being auctioned, but did get herself and Stone included in the group moving on to Brighton Hall in the morning, it would be enough. Once they were at Brighton Hall, her father would not be able to stop the mission. And once they were at Brighton Hall, Vaughn could pinpoint the secrets behind this particular auction.

Her father wanted her to pull out now. Stone would be happy if she retrieved as much intel as she could tonight and then let him follow up on it. Ling Mai was probably expecting a little more from Vaughn, but not much.

It was time to show them all that Vaughn had her own agenda and was quite capable of accomplishing it.

Showtime!

She smoothed damp palms along the front of her dress and paused at the open doorway between the hotel and the main verandah.

Stone should be waiting somewhere on the shadowed grounds before her, dotted with guests catching the evening coolness. It was the best place to find Blade, too. Though it was because of the first man and not the second that she had chosen this dress.

Another from her personal closet, one she'd bought on a whim sometime ago but never dared to wear. Until now.

It was a Donna Karan. Blood red. Plunging neckline. Cinched swatches of fabric draped across her waist, sweeping the ground even though she was wearing four-inch heels. Sensuous movement with every breath, though her breasts were thrust up and out in a way that made breathing a luxury.

There was nothing soft and silky about this dress, or the way she wore it. It screamed sex. Purred seduction. Promised heaven on the road to hell.

If she was going to be a lure, she might as well act like one. The mission was to extract intel, but she was going to proceed her way—not Stone's way.

She kept her hair down, thick and as dark as the velvet sky. It curled with the humidity yet still hung below her shoulders. She'd smudged her eye makeup, chosen glossy, sin red lipstick and, just to make sure, she'd wet her lips.

Stone, eat your heart out.

Wait. That was supposed to be Blade. Blade was the target. The one meant to fall hard and fast.

Keep focused, chiquita.

She inhaled all the way to her toes before stepping outside, aware of the stares of the other hotel patrons, the attention, the whispers.

With each step she took, she heard the swish of real silk stockings, the rasp of a garter along her inner thigh, thrummed with the cadence of her accelerating pulse.

For Blade. For Blade.

Make him want. Dare him. Let him know what he'd missed before and could get now, if he played the game.

Her game—her way.

But it was Stone's gaze locking with hers. Only his she heeded as she neared where he stood.

"How am I doing?" She kept her own gaze straight ahead as she brushed against his sleeve.

"I said lure, not lust."

Two days ago, she'd have heard a put-down. Tonight she heard only the growl. A low, primordial male sound heating her blood.

"I thought you wanted this wrapped up by the end of the night?" She raised one eyebrow as she accepted a glass of champagne from a passing waiter and returned his shy smile while glancing around for Blade.

"I hope the hell you know what you're doing." Stone's voice rasped against her nerves, whispering across her skin, as heat saturated the night air.

"I don't have to." She took a slow sip, tasting nothing, glancing at him over the rim of her glass. "That's what you're here for. Bait doesn't need to think."

His gaze darkened.

Heat lightning crackled on the horizon. Some looked up, but not her. Stone's gaze caught her as a firefly to the nearest light. The flicker of a candle from a nearby table cast angry shadows along the lines of his face.

If she was seduction tonight, he was temptation, and he did nothing more than look.

Was this how Eve fell? Satan smiled and she tumbled?

"Vaughn."

Her name being called from nearby broke the spell. Stone glanced away first, which gave her a second to gather her wits.

Games within games, and it'd pay her well to remember who were the pros.

"You look stunning," Blade said upon reaching her side.

She turned to smile at him, a smile she ratcheted up when she noted the hunger in his gaze.

Feeding time.

"Thank you." There was no need to say more.

"May I steal you for a moment?" Blade spoke not to her but to Stone. "If your husband approves."

For a moment, Stone's refusal hung in the balance, mirrored in the muscles of his face, the tension radiating from his stance, the flare of his nostrils.

Don't blow it, rock man.

"Sure, why not." His answer was accompanied by a shrug, an Academy Award–winning performance.

She shifted, making sure all her attention was focused on Blade now. Laying one hand on his sleeve, she lowered her voice, slowed its pace, nearly impossible with Stone listening and watching over her shoulder, waiting for her to push too far, to screw up.

But this was her world now, her abilities called to the fore, her experience in talking, laughing, wordplay with powerful, commanding men.

"Are you going to show me something interesting?" she purred.

Russian eyes narrowed and his hand slid over hers as he moved her deeper into the shadows before stopping. Not enough to trigger a woman's internal alarms, but enough to ensure privacy. His bodyguards hung back. Was it prearranged or were they astute?

"I believe you are wasted on your importer-exporter, my dear." Blade kept his tone light, the pressure of his hand heavy.

She laughed, a low bubbling sound. "I told you, M.T. has his uses."

"Like slapping your family's very public face?"

The question reminded her that this might be a game, but the players were very, very real. And possibly lethal.

"There, there, I see I have been crude," Blade crooned when she couldn't answer past the tightening of her throat. "It is wrong of me to, how you say, poke the fun?"

Play the game, Vaughn.

"It is naughty of you."

"Then I shall be naughty."

He could mean many things by his comment, none of them good, except Vaughn caught where his gaze rested, over her shoulder. On Stone.

"Did you wish to tell me something, Blade?" She heard the bite in her tone. So she wasn't as good a poker player as these two men, both able to check and hold their emotions as the stakes were raised.

Blade's smile told her he sensed her pique, if not the reason for it.

"I have been thinking about you today, Vaughn."

"Oh?"

"It has been too long since you have joined me and other members of the Attainment Club."

He waited a beat, eyeing her response.

Let him wait. Stone was right about this. Rushing her interest might scare off the prey.

"The club?" she asked, breaking the silence between them.

"You have forgotten so soon? I am surprised. Were our little auctions so unmemorable?"

"It is not that I have forgotten." *Reel him in slowly.* "It's just that I rarely choose to go backward, playing the games of childhood again."

"You no longer like the thrill?"

"Thrills change over the years, Blade. You of all people should know this."

"True. Very true."

Ouch. She read it in the tensing of his features, the curl of his hand upon her arm. There'd be bruises there tomorrow.

"You do not give me credit for increasing the stakes?" His breathing deepened.

She leaned forward, using her body to feign interest. "In what ways?"

"I, too, grew bored with the same old items."

"So?"

"So times have changed. I have changed. What is available for sale has changed."

Vaughn hoped Stone could hear every word through the watch transmitter she wore, a Bugatti style, not that cheap, commercial brand the tech group had designed.

Her game, her way.

"You are not very clear, Blade." She kept her words low. Whispered and intrigued. "What exactly are you saying?"

He bit, but only a little. "Mystery is its own seduction, my dear." He stepped closer and, with the hand not beneath his, she gripped her drink harder.

"Meaning?"

His laugh sent a wave of ice slithering down her spine.

"You are interested?" he asked.

"I might be."

"And your new husband?" Blade glanced toward the open grounds. "What of him?"

"What of him?" She offered a non-committal shrug.

"Is he to be trusted?"

"Not with your money or your wife, but with information, I'd say yes. If it is worth his while."

Blade's eyes narrowed. Obviously he'd come to a similar conclusion.

"He has the funds to play?"

Vaughn let her laugh ripple slowly before replying. "It is not funds that's the issue with M.T. He must be interested enough to play."

"And what interests your husband?"

She paused, as if debating how much to reveal. "Power. Ownership. Control." She sipped her drink and smiled. "Having what no one else can have."

That should cover all the bases, and sound enough like Blade to make her point.

"Then I believe he may be interested in *this* auction."

"Oh?"

"But it is not for the fainthearted."

Finally, something she could speak to from experience. "M.T. is not fainthearted."

"This is good. You will come then?"

"I still don't know what you will be auctioning."

Would getting the intel be enough? Would the mission be over if she did?

"Be my guest at Brighton Hall and you will find out."

She could almost hear Stone's voice. *Slowly. Don't push him too far too fast. Don't overstep.*

"And how shall I convince M.T.? He is already becoming bored with India. Until the monsoons come, this heat grows oppressive."

"He will not notice the heat higher in the hills."

"True." She shook her head. "For me, Blade, I would love to come. Just like old times. But I don't know about M.T."

"Then you must convince him. Believe me, it will be worth his time. Worth both your time." He stepped closer, leaning forward to brush a kiss across her temple. "We will start where we should never have stopped before."

Truth or dare? And why was it so hard to figure which side of the fence she'd land on? This was Blade. She owed him. But how far would she go to cancel her debt?

"Blade?" Her tone turned serious. "You know I'm your friend."

"Of course. Is this not what we're talking about?" His voice still flirted.

"I want you to know that you're important to me." *Or had been,* a small voice added.

But Blade wasn't interested in hearing about friendship. Not as he stepped closer, brushing against her. Funny. She didn't flinch as she would have had it been Stone.

"I want you to come tomorrow, Vaughn. Make it happen."

Russian czar to peasant.

Fine. Think about the mission. Not about Stone or Blade or friendships. Mission only.

She smiled; in the shadows, he would never be able to tell it didn't reach her eyes. "I'll talk to M.T., but he has no need of trinkets." Watching the furrows deepen in Blade's face, she added, "His words, not mine."

"I will not be offering trinkets."

"Can you not give me any more clues of what you will be offering?"

"Power, my dear. Life and death over hundreds of thousands. More, if one chooses."

Her stomach flip-flopped. Was this what an MI6 agent had died for? What could possibly offer such power? And what the hell was Blade involved in?

She moistened her lips. "That's a big promise, Blade."

"And one I'm able to supply. For the right incentive."

"Vaughn?"

It was Stone's voice, and it had never sounded so sweet.

Blade leaned closer to her, his breath brushing her ear. "Speak to your husband. I look forward to your arrival at Brighton Hall tomorrow."

He left then, nodding to Stone as they passed each other.

"You all right?" Stone asked after he made sure they were alone.

"Yes." *Be a professional. Professionals don't get spooked by words in the dark.* "Did you hear everything?"

"Yes."

"And?"

"I don't like the sound of things."

"I agree." The shiver she'd repressed earlier snaked through her. "So we go to Brighton Hall and find out what's being auctioned?"

"Unless you have a better way of getting the intel."

"No."

He looked past her to where Blade had disappeared into the hotel.

"Then we go to Brighton Hall."

The good news—the mission was on. The bad news—the mission was on.

Hadn't she learned years ago to be careful what she wished for?

Sometimes wishes became real.

Chapter 13

"Quite an illustrious group." Stone's voice was hushed, washed over by the sounds of arriving guests as they stood in the cavernous lobby of the Brighton Hall resort. They had not seen Blade since Vaughn's conversation the previous evening, but their host had been busy.

Kelly had confirmed that Stone's assumed identity had been researched, very thoroughly, over the past two days. And both Vaughn and Stone recognized the cameras monitoring all guest arrivals. A camera with a telltale addition allowing usage of facial recognition software. Very subtle. Very effective.

Vaughn kept her attention on the incoming guests, watching body language, memorizing who arrived with whom, a skill she'd learned at her mother's side during years of ambassadorial duties. Her father often joked that his wife intuitively knew more of what was happening around them than his security people did, and he was right.

Vaughn once asked her mother if that bothered her, her skills being used but never officially acknowledged. The look Vaughn received in return was pure don't-be-ridiculous. Vaughn's mother had been raised to be decorative, functional and invisible, skills Vaughn now mimicked even as she shielded her real intentions behind them.

"So what now?" Vaughn pitched her voice low as a precaution, though no other guest was near enough to hear.

Stone sidled up closer before answering. "Whatever Golumokoff is auctioning, it's attracting a very interesting crowd."

Damn, he smelled good.

Keep focused on the mission. The mission. The mission.

"Meaning?"

"Do you recognize any of his guests? Anyone from your set?"

"No." She ignored the words *her set*. "They are not the usual bored and jaded crowd. There's something different about these people."

"Soulless."

She glanced at him, stunned at the word, aware of how right on target it was.

"Good call," she murmured. "What are the implications?"

He nodded toward a tight-knit group of gentlemen and one woman just crossing the teak-walled foyer.

"Newest group is from mainland China. Involved in the suppression at Tiananmen Square a few years ago. The elderly gentleman who arrived earlier, Sun Yen from Taiwan, has been involved with nearly every large-scale arms brokering coming out of Southeast Asia since the seventies. There's also a certain oil-gorged sheikh with strong political leanings and Seamus O'Reilly, a member of the IRA with a very colorful and long-documented past."

"That's not soulless." Her breath hitched and held. "That's a tinderbox waiting for a match."

He offered a weary smile. "Your friend likes to play with a motley crew."

This so did not seem like her Blade. What was the man involved with and why? She continued to scan the crowd. "There are very few women."

"You noticed."

What did he think she was, a total idiot? On second thought, this was Stone.

"Give me some credit." She tried to step back but his hand anchored her in place. "Maybe others are already in their rooms."

"Possibly, but Alex's last contact noted little traffic in and out, except for the staff, until the last hour. I'd say our host would want most of his bidders to see the other bidders."

"Up the ante?"

"That'd be my guess. Did your friend indicate when the auction would take place?"

Was there emphasis on the word *friend?* What was Stone's game here—professional or personal? And why were the lines blurring?

"You heard everything I heard." Her words sounded hoarse.

"I didn't know if you'd had other contact with him. It'd be easy enough to lose track of loyalties in your situation."

She couldn't believe he was really saying that. This time, she shrugged off his nearness and stepped away, not far enough to cause anyone else to notice but enough to give her breathing room. "You think I'd tip off Blade as to why we're here?"

"You yourself said he was a compelling man. Money, power, looks. Besides, you owe him. Your words, not mine."

"Give me a break."

"We're a team here."

"And teams are supposed to trust each other." His own words thrust back at him. For love of money, the man was dense.

He was saved from responding by the arrival of a rotund man who could have passed for a Santa impersonator.

"Seamus O'Reilly." The man spoke with the lilt of an Irish tenor. "County Tyrone. I don't believe we've met."

Vaughn extended her hand as the newcomer could grow old and die before Stone made a move. "Good morning, I'm Vaughn and this is my husband." The word jammed in her throat. "M.T."

"Marcos," Stone clarified.

"Aye, and would that be the Marcos Stone involved in that little incident in the Moluccas about ten years ago?"

"Could be."

Vaughn kept her smile frozen in place as the Irishman sized up Stone before grinning. "That was a nice piece of work. Too bad what happened to the buyers later."

"Yeah. Too bad," came Stone's wooden reply.

Rock man to the fore.

"I see." Santa Seamus didn't look put off in the least as he turned to Vaughn. "Glad to see a pretty face among this lot. Golumokoff seems to have forgotten a few of the finer things in life with this here setup."

"So you've been to Blade's auctions before?" Vaughn asked.

"Heard about them," came the cagey reply. "The items haven't interested me much in the past, if you know what I mean." He winked at Stone, man to man.

"Not sure I do." Stone's deadpan response did serve a purpose. Once rude, one could remain rude. Too bad her background hadn't included such training. She could do snubs, slights and disdain—but not rude.

"Ah, so you're in the dark, too, as far as the details."

"Somewhat."

Their new best buddy edged closer. "I'll tell you my news if you tell me yours." He laughed roundly at his own wit. "If you know what I mean."

"Why don't you tell first?"

She had to give Stone credit. He was a pro at holding the upper hand.

The Irishman grinned and nodded. "Fair enough. Though I only know one word." He leaned in closer, waving Vaughn and Stone toward him. "Weaponry."

"Weaponry?" Vaughn glanced at Stone, who gave nothing away. As usual.

This was news. Bad news. *Blade, what are you doing?*

"Surprised you, did I now?" The man's smile widened. "It's your turn. Fair is fair."

Vaughn waited for Stone to take the lead, this time. He looked only at O'Reilly before saying, "Big."

"Big? What kind of information is that? Big."

Vaughn found it a challenge to keep a straight face. "That's all I have, friend. Big."

The Irishman looked disgusted. "As in size? Or potential? What?"

"Don't know. Guess we'll find out soon enough."

The other man shook his head and ambled off muttering, "Big."

"You'd make a poor diplomat." Vaughn kept her gaze averted.

"Thought I did just fine. Revealed nothing, learned something new."

"A big ugly something."

"Did you think we were going to find out good news about your friend, princess?" His look darkened, became more intense, if that were possible. "You still want to believe he's simply a misunderstood soul who's trying his best in an impossible world."

"Back off, Stone." She'd thought they'd moved beyond this, but for some reason Stone had a burr up his backside and he was taking it out on her. Not teamwork by her definition of the word. "I'm going to the room."

She didn't wait for a reply. When she reached the elegant accommodations, she barely looked at the rich hand-knotted rugs, teak furniture and *jamewar*-draped bed coverings, but went directly to the balcony offering a vista of Himalayas all around.

"Alex?" She activated the communicator hidden in her watch. "Can you copy?"

She waited a moment before trying again, not unclenching shoulders until the telltale static indicated a reply.

"Jayleen here. What's up?"

Not the comfy support person she'd hoped for.

"You on a secure channel?"

Vaughn listened to a click or two before Jayleen's voice returned. "All our friends are off. What's up?"

"We've heard the item may involve weaponry."

"What kind?"

Give us a break, we just arrived.

Vaughn bit her tongue before replying. "No other details. Other players include mainland Chinese, Taiwanese and an IRA connection."

Jayleen whistled before asking, "You have specific names?"

No. Vaughn had come here expecting to talk to Alex, a little pick-me-up connection, not to give a full-scale report. But she wasn't about to tell Jayleen that.

"We'll have a longer report this evening. Just wanted to give a heads-up."

"Makes sense," came the cryptic response.

"What makes sense?"

"Your card today."

Oh crap, not this again. First the poor woman facing piercing swords, then death. How much more fun could Jayleen whip up for Vaughn with her bloody tarot cards? There was only one way to nip this nonsense in the bud.

"Out for now—"

"Wait." Jayleen's voice sounded desperate.

Vaughn sucked in a lungful of pine-scented air. "You're going to make me listen whether I want to or not."

"For your own good, girl."

Yeah, right, and if she believed that she'd believe she and Stone were a well-oiled team. "Spit it out, I don't have much time."

"The grail. Reversed."

As if that meant something? Maybe Vaughn could slide by with having just listened. "Thanks, Jayleen, gotta go—"

"The grail is about a quest, the energy and desire that each of us chases."

That didn't sound too bad.

Jayleen's voice continued, "Reversed, it means confused priorities. Obsession."

She should have cut this conversation short.

"Fine. Duly noted."

"You watch yourself, Vaughn."

Great, watch for Blade to auction who knew what, watch the mission shift and change, watch Stone not quite trusting her and now she had to watch herself.

"Over and out."

She ended the transmission on Jayleen's sputter. Served the woman right, stirring up trouble when Vaughn needed her focus to be clear and single-minded.

The transmitter on her wrist buzzed. Clicking the incoming line open came as an automatic response.

"Vaughn?" It was Jayleen, but not pissed like Vaughn expected. Cool maybe, but not bitch-slapping pissed. Yet.

"Yes?"

"They found the second agent this morning."

"And?"

"This one had been tortured before being put out of his misery."

"Got it." What more could she say? She was heart-sick at the news.

This time Jayleen severed the connection.

Vaughn stood on the balcony for a few moments, deeply inhaling the cool mountain air when she heard Stone arrive. He'd have to be told, but she hesitated. Self-preservation, no doubt. No point in handing him more ammunition to oust her from the mission at this time. Twenty-four hours and they'd have the answers they'd come for. She hoped.

He said nothing as he joined her, standing just behind her, looking out over the peaks. He stood so close the give and take of his breathing whispered across her, the warmth of his skin seeped into her.

"I was out of line back there."

It was the last thing she had expected from him.

She made to turn, but his hands on her shoulders stopped her. She should have protested but didn't. Why?

"You were right." His words brushed against her. "I should have trusted you a little more."

"Could you repeat that?"

"Don't push it, princess."

She couldn't help but grin. She really couldn't, in spite of the fact his hands dropped. Too bad the tension remained wire tight between them.

"So what now, Kemo Sabe?" *Keep it light. Keep it professional.*

"We found one clue. Time to find more." He hesitated, as if meaning to say more but catching himself.

"Divide and conquer?" she asked.

"Just stay out of trouble."

"I always do."

"I'm not as gullible as your Russian boyfriend."

"True." She turned then, still surprised how good his earlier words had sounded. "Any advice on approach?"

"It'd be smarter to ask fewer questions up front," he said, treating her like a true teammate for once. "Get a feel for the people and the place before we start pushing too deep."

"How much time do you think we have?"

"Not much, but I do know one thing."

"And that is?"

"If Golumokoff's weaponry is on site, it's not very large."

"Is this good news?"

"Not necessarily. But there's no point in spending too much time speculating. Let's start asking a few well chosen questions."

"Fine."

"And princess."

"Yeah?"

"Stay safe."

He hesitated again, but offered nothing more.

She'd tell him about the second MI6 agent later, hopefully offsetting the bad news with some other good news about exactly what Blade was involved in.

It was hours later when Vaughn had to admit to herself just how hard it was to extract intel from people who lived in the shadows. These were not the folks her parents entertained at ambassadorial functions.

She met with Stone before entering the open-walled restaurant set up for the evening banquet, the smells of roasted meat and curries wafting around them. He looked the same as when she'd left him—nothing out of place, aloof and in control—but he wasn't happy.

"You playing angel to your vamp of the other day," he remarked as she approached.

The comment was classic rock man as his gaze skimmed over her Vera Wang taupe silk taffeta-draped gown, with a sequined bra and cap sleeves. Skimmed and lingered at the scoop of her neckline, leaving her pulse skipping into overtime.

The rest of the dress, shades of cream and off-white, might look demure and tame, but not the neckline.

"Either you need a stiff drink or food to fuel you." She looked beyond him, not really seeing anything. "Keep it up, Stone, you actually sound like a grumpy husband."

"God forbid." He took her bare arm, his fingers sure and warm against her skin, and steered her toward the restaurant, giving her one last sizzling glance, making her wonder anew what it'd be like between them if there were no mission. "You sure you don't have a shawl or sheet or something to drape across what you're wearing, or have you forgotten you're in the minority here and most of these fellows are not Cub Scouts?"

"Have you forgotten you can get further with honey than with vinegar? Quit growling."

"I don't growl."

She never would have believed Stone could do sulky little boy. He really was out of sorts. Or worried.

"I take it you found out as much as I did." The swell of conversations, in several languages, made talking close to one another easier to get away with. And focusing on what they were here for kept her heartbeat steadier.

"It's a weapon, or involved with weaponry, and comes out of the former Soviet Union, which makes sense." He scanned the room, always on watch, always wary. "That, and the fact it's expected to have a hefty price tag. You?"

"Ditto. Only other fact is that there's a time element involved."

"How so?" he asked.

"Couldn't find specific details, but whatever *it* is *must* be used in the near future."

"Not a good phrase."

They could say no more as a bronze gong was rung and guests started taking their seats around a table King Arthur would have envied. Vaughn silently complimented Blade for his political astuteness. There could be few ruffled feelings about seating arrangements when everyone had an equal place at the round table and he also allowed guests who might not otherwise see or recognize one another a fine opportunity to do so over the meal. The better to whet their appetites for the bidding later, no doubt.

It wasn't until near the end of the third course that their host joined them.

A swell of greetings announced his arrival, and no one could miss the storm trooper bodyguards flaring out in front of him. More muscle here than in the more public and vulnerable Hotel Taj.

Interesting. One might think Blade did not trust some, or most, of his guests.

But then, he'd always been a very smart man.

If she thought the show was going to begin with his arrival, she was mistaken. He played the part of congenial ringmaster very well, laughing and smiling, acknowledging certain individuals with a nod here, a smile there. His gaze caught and held Vaughn's as he raised a glass of exquisite Bordeaux to his lips.

She replied in kind, toasting him even as Stone stiffened at her side. The game had begun in earnest and they were now playing their parts. Hard to do, as Stone's arm brushed against her time and time again.

The man didn't betray nerves even here, sipping rarely and eating lightly. She wondered if he made love with as much restraint, or if there he'd finally let go.

"You're smiling," he whispered at her side.

Did the man miss anything?

"It's a very good meal."

He nodded, but his eyes called her a liar.

Good thing Blade chose that moment to stand and tap his glass with a fork.

The crowed stilled, but there remained a hum in the air, the energy of suppressed emotions tinder tight and ready to ignite.

"I wish to thank you all for joining me here today." Several heads nodded. "Some old friends and acquaintances. Many new faces. But only a few who will walk away with the opportunity I will be providing. The pièce de résistance of this gathering."

Stone whispered to her, "The man would have made a great used car salesman."

She had to agree. Blade understood the power of hype, the thrill of anticipation, and he played the crowd for all it was worth.

"Tonight is for relaxation." Blade smiled. "Tomorrow is for business."

A few groans rumbled beneath the other talk.

He nodded in acknowledgment. "Do not worry. It will be worth your time. For now, enjoy."

The man was going to draw out their wait even more.

"What now?" she asked Stone, leaning toward him.

"We return to our room."

That was the master plan? Hurry up and wait?

"Patience," he said at her side as he rose from his seat.

That mind-reading talent could get real old real quick.

"I *am* patient."

"Yeah, and I'm flexible." The grin he gave her had her wondering if he had made a joke.

"Vaughn?" Blade materialized behind her chair.

Great. She'd been so focused on Stone she'd totally lost track of keeping an eye on the prize.

"You have us intrigued." She gathered together what shreds of thoughts she could find as she stood, crumpling her napkin before sliding it onto the table. "And, as usual, you throw a very nice gathering."

"Nice?"

Vaughn glanced around the table at the retreating guests before replying. "Let's say it's a different crowd than I expected."

"I told you, times have changed." He turned to include Stone in the conversation. "I hope you are enjoying yourself?"

"I'm here."

If she had to learn patience, someone else had to learn politeness.

She cleared her throat, hoping to deflect any swords about to be drawn. Blade didn't seem to mind as he smiled, a shark's look, more of a razor-edged grin than a smile. Rudeness must be a guy thing.

Blade was looking at her once again. "Perhaps we can talk tomorrow."

"Before or after the auction?" she asked.

"Let's make it before. Say ten. At the infinity pool. Just the two of us."

"I look forward to it." There was no protest from Stone. Maybe they were making progress.

"Till later." Blade nodded at her first, then Stone. "Adieu."

She watched him walk away and caught Stone watching her.

"What?" She leaned toward him, even though the dinner guests had already dispersed. "Just because you don't know how to play nice."

"We're not here to play nice."

"Then you get high scores." She pushed her chair back to move around him. "I'll see you in the room. Later."

There. She was learning. If Stone could take potshots and walk away, so could she. In fact, she might actually get good at it. With enough practice. And with Stone around, she figured there'd be plenty of practice.

Chapter 14

When she returned to the room, she was surprised to find it empty. If Stone was trying to one-up her by staying out later, let him. After she had spent the evening talking to what seemed like every slimeball and international criminal on the face of the earth, he was welcome to chat up the rest as much as he wanted. Whatever Blade was going to present tomorrow, he was keeping it under wraps.

On the other hand, Stone could be staying away to keep up the pretense that all was not well in the honeymoon suite. It'd worked fine so far—she complaining of a headache one night, two nights of Stone picking a minor spat before bedtime, all for the listening ears. But that could be continued only so long.

"Here."

Stone's voice came from the balcony. She followed it, not surprised to see him blending so well with the shadows.

"What's up?" She made sure she kept her voice low, in case there were other neighbors enjoying the late-night coolness. No heat lightning tonight, just a million stars in a jet black bowl of sky.

"No bugs out here," he clarified for her as she joined him, though speaking on the balcony hadn't been an issue so far. It was the one place Blake's goons didn't bug.

"We have a job. Two."

Finally. Something other than schmoozing. If that was all she'd wanted to do, she'd have stayed in her parents' world.

"You contacted Alex?"

"Yes. Ling Mai wants us to bug Golumokoff's place and also wants us to insert tracking devices on several of the other guests."

"On them?"

"On articles of clothing or something they might use on a regular basis."

"Like a wristwatch or in a cell phone?"

"Exactly."

"When and how?"

"Now." He glanced over their rail, into the midnight darkness. Their room was on the highest level, four stories up, with a three-story drop below them.

"I'll take the Russian's room. You take these three others."

She glanced at the scrap of paper he handed her. "Why are you taking Blade? You have more experience and are quicker than I am. You'd be able to cover these gentlemen, and I use the term loosely, faster than I ever could. Also, the locks on Blade's rooms are an older version. Quite easy to pick with my tools."

"You managed to smuggle them in?"

"I have them incorporated into a chunky necklace. No one looks at it twice."

"Smart lady. Fine. You take Golumokoff."

She'd expected more of a protest from him. Maybe they were making progress. At least professionally.

Then he added, "Get in and get out. Nothing fancy."

"I don't do fancy. My instructor never taught me."

She could have sworn his lips twitched, but his tone was serious when he spoke again. "I mean it, Vaughn. In and out. No heroics. It's not worth it."

He'd called her by her name. A first, but now was not the time to dwell on the slight slip.

"Sure. You give the orders, I follow them."

"Like I believe that."

There was no point in saying anything else. Time was being wasted.

It took her less than twenty minutes to change from haute couture to thief black. A silk turtleneck, hiding as much skin as possible, slim-legged pants, crepe soles with Velcro closures to easily slip on and off and the prerequisite black ski mask to hide facial glare. All items hidden in plain sight, with other outdoor wear suitable for a ski trip in the lower Himalayas. She twisted her hair in a French braid, and her pulse was steady. As steady as could be expected, given the assignment.

At last she was doing what she'd wanted to do. Make a difference, use new skills, be alive. The rush was unbelievable.

"You know where the Russian is?" Stone asked, as if rethinking the assignments.

"The last time I saw him, he was talking with a group in one of the side rooms." She kept her voice calm and modulated, nothing like her pulse. "It looked like it'd be a long conversation."

"Remember. Get in—"

"And get out. Thanks, I got it."

"You will get it if I have to save your scrawny hide."

"Oh, and here I thought you cared." She was pushing buttons, but it wasn't often she got to tease Stone. Never, actually, and it had its own masochistic thrill. "Forty minutes tops. No more."

"See you then."

Her modified canvas ALICE vest with its multiple pockets held the devices to be planted and a krypton flashlight. Her Swiss seat harness and carabiners were checked and double-checked.

If caught, she'd have to rely on the blade strapped to her ankle and the moves Stone had taught her over the past weeks. She hoped it was enough.

Stepping to the balcony, she untwisted a short length of nylon rope. Earlier it'd been twined around a native rug she'd picked up in the market, a good disguise and easily overlooked by the goons scanning their luggage as they arrived.

The nylon whistled through her hands as she fed it over the rail, tightened her waist harness and cinched her safety knot. The wind chilled her face; goose bumps climbed up her spine.

"Here goes nothing."

Swinging her first leg over the rail was the hardest. During the day, one could see the sheer drop from where the hotel perched on a cliff. At night, it was worse, inky blackness yawning at her like the mouth of hell.

"You're not a quitter," she reminded herself, but silently, in case Stone was still hanging around.

The second leg was easier. A slight breeze swirled around her, enough to cool the sweat beading her forehead, but not enough for her to have to adjust her trajectory.

She pushed off lightly, aware she had to clear the windows of the room directly below hers and touch down only on the thin slate cladding between stories.

Her parents' world was forgotten; her new world consumed her. The stakes were high. Screw up here, and not only would she and Stone suffer, but also the team and the Agency.

She tightened her hold as her shoes thudded firmly yet silently against the siding, reminding her to inhale between swings. Two floors more to go brought her level with the balcony she needed. It wasn't like Blade to take a lesser room, but this time it seemed to suit his purposes.

The interior was stygian dark. She hoped that was

because he was still playing host and not because he had returned to the room early. With a pause outside the balcony door, scanning through paned windows, she crouched down to examine the lock, using her flashlight as little as possible.

The lock was as she had described it to Stone. The interior ones leading from the hallway were keyless entry pads, but no one had thought to change the locks on the exterior doors. Probably figured no fool would want to scale this high up a cliff face to reach the resort in the first place.

She glanced behind her, listening to the wind picking up in intensity as it stole through the nearest treetops. Treetops *below* her.

Showtime!

Picking the lock took less than two minutes. With a gentle push she opened the door, damming her breath with the movement, and paused.

Stillness.

No breathing from the bed. Nothing except the ticking of a clock.

All clear.

She closed the balcony door behind her softly. Her shoes made no noise as she crossed the Bokhara rug to the far door, the one leading to the main hallway.

Her heart slammed into her ribs as she heard voices on the other side, then slowed its beat as she realized it was two guards talking to each other. Nothing more.

She crept away, giving a quick peek into the bathroom. Empty.

Stone had given her three listening devices. Newer versions that did not need an electrical connection as older models had. No light sockets and switches for these puppies; they could be inserted anywhere.

She scanned the room before moving.

The first bug went at the end of the bed, almost dead center in the room. The second device fitted nicely near the dresser, where Blade's briefcase lay locked. The third. Where should the third go?

She chose the briefcase, knowing it was a bit dicey. She inserted it on the base, hoping it worked as well as the techs had promised.

She hesitated. This was Blade. He had saved her once and now she was repaying him by spying on him? If Stone and Ling Mai were right, then Blade deserved it. But if they were wrong, she was betraying a friend, one she still owed.

It was then that she heard the sound. Voices raised on the other side of the main door.

Blade was back.

A quick scan. Not enough time to make the balcony. No room beneath the bed. Bathroom too small.

Damn and double damn.

Every childhood horror movie she'd ever watched flashed before her.

When in doubt—

She ducked behind the window draperies as the door swung open. Blade was silhouetted by the hallway light, turned away from her.

He spoke guttural Russian to the two men beyond him.

If he as much as glanced at the window, she was a goner. She splayed her feet sideways, hoping the material did not sway, praying he'd cross to the bathroom before doing anything else.

If he found her, Stone would kill her. No, wait, Blade would kill her first, *then* go after Stone. Neither was a good scenario.

The light blazed on, mimicking midday in August. No wimpy watt bulbs in this hotel.

Bathroom. Bathroom. Go to the bathroom.

Blade's feet crossed to where the briefcase lay. Then paused.

Bathroom.

She could hear the slight click of the lock on his case opening. The sound of it being laid against the dresser.

For the love of God, go to the bathroom.

His cell phone rang.

Didn't the man have a bladder? If he were a woman, he'd have been in and out by now.

He spoke, Italian this time. She could make out a few words. Not many, but maybe, if she lived, she'd have some news to share with Stone.

A big *if.*

Something about Lake Como. He had a home there, that she remembered, but the conversation could be about anything. He spoke too fast for her to catch more than a few phrases.

Blade hung up.

Then nothing. Total silence. Her breath backed up in her lungs. She was sure her pounding pulse could be heard, sure this whole wanting-to-do-something-vital-with-her-life theory was a big mistake.

If he as much as glanced at the window, he'd be able to see the rope dangling there, lighter than the darkness around it. When would they start making black nylon rope?

He cleared his throat; a cannon blast at close range would have been quieter.

Then he moved.

Toward her? She strained to hear. Hard to do when pinpricks of light danced in her vision from lack of oxygen.

Then she heard it. The click of the bathroom door.

She counted to three, then peered out.

Nothing. It was closed.

She stepped back, opened the balcony door and closed it. Five more beats to grab the rope and hand over hand pull herself out of sight of the window.

Only then did she start breathing again.

She'd done it. If she could have released one hand long enough to punch it in the air, she would have. Instead, she clenched them both tighter around the nylon rope.

Sweat cooled in the hollow of her back. From fear? Exaltation? Both?

She could hardly wait to tell Stone; she'd done it.

One hand over the next, she climbed higher.

Payback was going to be sweet.

Chapter 15

"You're late."

Good thing Stone waited until she had at least one leg swung over the rail before scaring the bejabbers out of her.

"Anyone tell you not to hide in the dark and scare people?"

She swung the other leg over, unhooking her rope and harness.

"I said forty minutes. It's been fifty-two." He stepped from where he'd been leaning against the far balcony rail.

"Don't get anal on me, Stone. It's been a long night already. I'm here now. Job's done. An attagirl would be appreciated."

"I don't give attagirls when you screw up."

Oh, that was choice. But what had she expected? A pat on the back might have been nice. A simple question or two about how she'd accomplished her goal. Something. Anything. Except this.

Then she heard the fear beneath his anger. For her? Or for the mission? Did it matter?

She wrapped the rope in a small coil, her heart still pounding, her breathing still too shallow and fast.

"Look, there was a complication." She tried to use routine to harness the rush still humming through her veins. "But it's all taken care of now."

"What complication?" He stepped closer.

Leave it to him to focus on that little detail.

"Nothing I couldn't handle."

She turned to enter the room but he stepped in front of her.

Not a wise move. Not with the adrenaline coursing through her system with the force of Niagara Falls.

"What complication?"

A smart person would have been afraid of his tone.

"I said I handled it."

So, she wasn't smart.

"Princess."

She stepped forward until she stood so close her breasts butted his chest. Daring him. Wanting him to push back so she could release some of the energy pumping through her at Mach 3.

By the flare of his nostrils, he knew it, too.

"Blade showed up." She ground each word from between clenched teeth. Her jaw would ache in the morning. "I was in the room. He went into the bathroom. I left. End of story."

Was that going to be good enough for rock man?

No. Of course not.

He raised his hand. Her breath hitched, waiting for a blow, surprised that he'd lose control.

But leave it to him to do the unexpected.

Instead of a swing, he brushed a wisp of hair from her cheek that had untangled from her braid. A slow sensation of touch rippling like wildfire through her.

That quickly the air escaped, replaced by the fear she'd experienced earlier but couldn't afford to acknowledge.

"I told you to be careful." His words washed against her, husky and deep.

"Yeah, but you didn't give the message to Blade."

He laughed then. A real laugh, if a bit rusty and one touching something so deep inside her it ached. An awareness, a need to see this man laugh more, to let down his guard, at least around her.

"Damn you, princess." And then he kissed her.

Not like in front of Ling Mai and the others, but softly, tenderly.

She expected fire from this man, sparks and heat and passion. Not gentleness.

She leaned into it. Found the kiss as welcoming as a warm blanket on a frigid night and as tempting.

She'd been afraid. So very afraid. Every step of the way from her first arrival at The Farm for training to the slow glide down the nylon rope.

But she could not admit it aloud and stay an agent for long.

And he seemed to sense that. With words unspoken, wrapping his arms around her, pulling her along the length of his hard, lean body, he offered just what she needed right then. A way to slow her racing pulse, a mindless drop. A physical release.

He deepened the kiss and she danced after it.

The man was meant to kiss. Lord, was he meant to.

She heard a soft moan, surprised it was hers, not surprised when he waltzed her back into the room, her knees hitting the back of the bed. No words were necessary. No trappings of romance and seduction.

It was inevitable. They'd poked and circled and snarled and hungered since the first day they had met. Two wary strangers fighting an attraction neither wanted nor sought.

It was inevitable.

And it was right.

He took his time, touching and tasting, guiding and gentling every raw nerve until she didn't know anything except him. There was room for no more.

She wanted his taste on her tongue, in her pores. Each rasp of skin against skin made the ache within more taut. Murmurs gave way to groans, need building, want replacing sanity.

He sheathed himself and she hesitated, wanting to tell him she didn't need protection. But this was Stone; it was what he did.

When they joined, it wasn't with a roar or crash but

the melding of sunset into the night sky. Rightness. Perfectly right and meant to be.

Inevitable.

It wasn't until later, much later, as she lay in the bed, the sheets scrunched at her feet, watching the brush of dawn across her skin, that she realized what had happened.

She glanced at him, his eyes closed, his face as rough-hewn and as tempting in sleep as it was in waking.

His breathing sounded even. Smooth and restful, even as hers jammed somewhere south of her breastbone.

She rose, shaky and unsteady, not wanting to acknowledge what had happened and the complications it created. But like a burr on a sock, it clung, refusing to be kicked free.

Deal with it.

The rug felt deep and thick beneath her feet as she padded into the bathroom, turning on cold water to splash onto her face, grabbing a towel to cover her nudity. Aware of a chill that had nothing to do with the morning temperature but that was seeping from her heart. She turned the shower on high, letting the steam fog the mirror.

You're a big girl, Vaughn, play it cool. It was an itch that had wanted scratching. Nothing but a need met, oh so well.

She caught herself smiling. When she glanced up from the sink he was there, behind her, watching her, his gaze no longer dark and heavy-lidded but intense and wary. Familiar, yet different.

He said nothing, but simply stood there, the sheet draped across his waist, his torso lean and muscled in the dawn's soft light. Even as she looked, she hungered for him again and for that alone she hesitated.

With the water still running she could speak, not loudly, but what she wanted to say didn't have to take long.

She kept her voice calm, her emotions jangling but in a different way than last night.

"Sleep well?" she asked, turning to splash cold water against her face.

He stepped closer and his scent reached her. Encircled her with the steam and the heat and the want.

She said nothing more as she turned, stepped closer and undid the knot holding the sheet in place. His nostrils flared; his voice was raw as he laughed.

"You're insatiable," he murmured, his lips skimming her jaw, nibbling her ear.

"Yeah." It came on a huff of breath.

"We've got work to do," he whispered in her ear, but his remark held no force.

"Later." It was her turn to laugh, and to waltz him back toward the shower.

He made no protest as he joined her.

At last, he was letting her lead.

Smart man.

Chapter 16

Vaughn waited until Stone left the room before she released the sigh she'd been holding. A coward's way? Maybe. But she needed the few minutes alone to settle nerve endings still humming.

God, she'd been easy.

Thank heavens. Another smile skimmed her lips, a satisfied, cat-licking-cream smile. If Stone ever saw it she'd never hear the end of it.

"So what now?" she asked herself.

The mission had changed, become complicated, though she doubted either of them wanted to deal with that issue right now. Not before the auction. Before her meeting with Blade.

It was just sex.

Nothing more.

Liar.

Okay, so it was mind-blowing, catch-your-breath-and-hold-on sex. And she wanted more. Lots more.

Not the issue.

So what was the issue? In a few minutes, she was heading down to meet Blade. A meeting that could change everything for him, and for her, forever. If he was innocent of what Ling Mai and Stone thought he was up to, she had a chance to stop him, *now,* before the situation got any dicier.

And if he was guilty? If he really was involved in the deaths of two MI6 agents and was indeed planning to auction a deadly weapon to the highest bidder—and all the facts pointed to that—then she was going to have to take him down. Destroy a friend. It was what she'd come to do, no matter what the cost.

She wasn't a quitter, no matter how tempting it'd be to walk out the main resort doors and never look back.

So that left only one alternative.

Time to be the professional she'd been training to become. Sex with Stone was a complication, but it had nothing to do with the mission.

She hoped.

She nudged aside the thought. No time or place for it. Not now.

Not ever.

Now she had a mission to complete and a man to meet.

Before she reached the door, her ear mike buzzed. An incoming communication from the team.

She headed toward the balcony before responding, hoping like Hades it wasn't Jayleen with another one of her tarot card warnings.

"I'm here." She kept her voice low as she hit the transmit function.

"Alex here."

"What's up?" It had to be important to break pattern and instigate a call.

"Uncle Charlie has sent several cousins snooping around."

Damn and double damn. CIA agents. Her father's people.

"How visible?"

"Mandy spotted two yesterday in Simla. Kelly caught sight of one closer to where you are."

Not good. If her team could spot the agents, it was a safe bet Blade's people could, too. Would their presence be enough to spook him into canceling the auction? Or would Blade assume the agents were connected with her in some way?

Really not good.

"Copy." She sighed. There wasn't a lot she could do on the inside, except find out what was being auctioned as soon as possible. Now her meeting with Blade took on a greater urgency. Save a friend or crucify him?

"You there, Vaughn?" Alex asked, her own voice distorted.

"Yeah, still here."

"Ling Mai wants your meeting with Blade on record."

Great. Complication on complication.

"And she wants to know ASAP what's being auctioned. Preferably before the auction goes down."

As if Vaughn and Stone didn't want the same thing.

"One other thing," Alex continued. "Weather front moving in, potential disruption to communication possible."

Vaughn glanced at the far horizon, seeing for the first time the gunmetal clouds marching toward them. Monsoon season. The first blast of wet brought relief, but at a price. Usually a blast of weather—winds, sheets of water, howling nature—tearing into everything in its path.

Maybe she should have been happy to get another of Jayleen's doom-and-gloom predictions.

"Oh, and Vaughn?" Alex's voice brought her back to the here and now.

"More good news?" came her slightly cynical response.

Alex didn't laugh. Instead she uttered a pithy, "Watch your back."

The communication cut out.

Vaughn squared her shoulders, smelling the scent of rain in the thick air. She was still early for her meeting with Blade, but the clock was ticking.

Friend or foe?

One thing was sure—she'd never find out hiding in her bedroom. Ling Mai wanted answers. Vaughn wanted, if possible, to save a friend. If he still was a friend.

It was time to act.

* * *

Blade joined her at the infinity pool on the southeast terrace. The view from here was even more spectacular than from other locations around the resort. Maybe it was the combination of blue, blue water silently gliding off the edge of the pool into open space, with the vista of row upon row of mountains, with tumbling storm clouds hugging their flanks in the background. It gave a sense of space and size that made a human appear puny and unimportant.

As if she didn't already.

"You look pensive." Blade reached for her hand, turning it and kissing the inside of her palm.

On any other day, and from any other man, it would have been salve to her wounds. Today, it was business.

"A long night." She kept her gaze averted.

"Trouble in paradise?"

"No."

"I am glad to see your husband not with you this morning."

"You asked to meet alone. Besides, we are not joined at the hip."

"I see." He came to stand beside her, shoulders brushing, gaze scanning the far horizons.

"Did you wish to meet to speak of my husband?" she asked when Blade made no move to speak. So what if the words came out a little acerbic. If Stone was listening, let him make his own guesses as to why; Alex or others on the other end of the watch transmitter could come to their own conclusions.

Blade smiled at her. He really did have fine eyes. She'd thought so the first time she'd seen him in Denmark all those years ago and nothing had changed.

"There may be a small adjustment to plans," he murmured, catching her off guard.

"About the auction?"

"No. The auction will proceed as planned."

"I don't understand."

"My team has concerns. About security."

Her heart dropped, a disconcerting experience when standing on the edge of the world.

"Is there a problem?"

"Nothing that cannot be handled."

Lord, he sounded like Stone now.

"Then the auction will continue?" She kept her tone light and casual.

"It will, though not as originally planned. An initial auction will be held here as my men search for suspected intruders. A second, final auction will be held elsewhere."

This was news. She hoped Alex was getting it all.

She probed. "Surely the whole group will not be moving?"

"There can always be another auction. Not like this one, but enough to keep all my special guests happy. They will not cause problems."

Was this good news, or not good news?

She was not dealing well with ambiguity this morning.

"Are you saying I'm causing you problems here, Blade?"

"You should never have gone away before. It was a mistake."

So Stone was right about where the Russian was coming from. Chalk one up for the rock man.

"We were traveling different paths." How was that for a noncommittal comment? Maybe Stone was rubbing off on her. Not a good thought as it conjured up the texture of his skin on hers, his scent mingling with hers, his heartbeat keeping pace beat for beat with hers.

Damn the man.

But there was one way to get the thoughts of one man out of your head when you were with another. She brushed her fingers against her watch, effectively silencing the communication. What she had to say next was not for public consumption. It was a risk, but it was her risk.

"Blade," she said, stepping closer, facing him now, sincere concern in her voice. "I need to know something."

"What?"

"This auction. These people." She waved a hand to indicate the guests beyond the glass doors. "I don't understand any of this. This is not like you. Or the you I knew."

"We all change, Vaughn."

"But there are rumors of weapons. Of the possibility of people being killed. Is that what you want?"

"You of all people should know how little one gets to do what they want." His laugh did not reach his eyes. "Come, Vaughn, what are you saying?"

She braced herself. "I'm worried about you. About what you're involved in."

"And yet you married Marcos Stone."

Crap. There was that.

"I married the man, not his business." Good thing she learned tap dancing as well as ballet.

But something in Blade's expression remained distant. Had she blown it? Or was he hearing what she needed him to hear?

She stepped closer still, resting one hand on his arm. Friend to friend. "I mean it, Blade. This isn't about Stone. This is about you. I owe you."

"For Copenhagen?"

"Yes." Her voice dropped. "For Copenhagen and for being a friend."

"Is that what I am to you?"

There was no script for this. Her training taught her not to dangle too far out on a limb, but her gut equated risk with reward. One did not grasp the brass ring without leaning far out on a whirling carousel horse.

She glanced toward the Himalayas, their peaks clear in the high air. "Yes, you're my friend and I want to help."

"I am not a man who needs help."

Now he was sounding like Stone. Lord save her from stubborn men who thought they had all the answers.

"Are you sure?" She looked up at him, wanting to shake and hug him at the same time. "Sometimes we can get in over our heads and don't know how to get out." Boy, was that true. "I just want to let you know I'm here for you."

"Are you?"

That didn't sound good. Had she gone too far? Given away too much? One would have thought working with

Stone over the last weeks would have taught her some measure of self-preservation. But then her mother had always said she had to push everything.

Her hand slid from Blade's arm. Time to get the mission back on track. Or maybe her focus. Forget saving Blade, or herself. She'd tried it her way. Now it was time to meet Ling Mai's objective.

"Speaking about the auction," she said, stepping the teeniest bit away from Blade, "what happens with it?"

"What do you mean?"

"I mean, you're talking about dealing with something very dangerous and very illegal. Aren't you concerned about repercussions?"

Nothing like baiting the bear and from the frown marring Blade's patrician face, she'd pushed his buttons.

"What type of repercussions?" His accent thickened with each word. Did pissing off the target come under risk-taking behavior or suicide? Was this the best way to find out what was being auctioned?

"Nothing specific." She shrugged, though her shoulders felt like lead weights. "But from meeting some of your other guests—" she glanced back at the hotel "—these are not the kind of people one wants as enemies."

"And you think they are my enemies?"

There was no avoiding his stare, or the intensity of it. Maybe it was a talent she had, of ticking off ruthless, emotionless, powerful men. Would Ling Mai see this as an attribute or a failure? Forget Ling Mai; how was Vaughn going to use it?

"Blade." She stepped closer and laid one hand across his tensed arm. "It doesn't matter what I think because I don't have enough information." In for a penny… "And until I do have enough information, how am I to make a decision about what you're involved with?"

Time beat one shudder at a time as she waited for Blade's response.

When it came, it surprised her.

"Come." He grabbed her arm, giving her no option. "I show you."

She skipped to keep up with him as he entered the hotel then veered left, heading toward the guest rooms.

"Blade, where—"

"Wait. You shall see."

It looked like she had little choice as he waved to his security guards, a double set, to fall in behind them. Through the foyer and past the startled hotel staff and one or two guests, down a hallway toward his room.

His expression was intense, his stride purposeful. That fast the easy camaraderie had changed between them. Or had it been there at all? This was not Blade her friend, this was the Russian Blade. The ruthless one.

When would she learn to stop pushing?

Had he found the bugs she had planted last night? Was it all over before it even began? Why had she turned off her communications device?

If it had been left on, at least someone would know how she died.

Chapter 17

Questions whirred like rotor blades with each step she skipped beside Blade. What was happening? Where was Stone? Was this the end?

"You are very quiet." Blade glanced her way as they reached his room and kept walking.

Good news or bad?

When in doubt, bluff. Had Stone taught her that? No, Mary Jo Lewinsky in sixth grade when they'd been caught sneaking into the dormitory at St. Margaret's Hall. It had worked then; it might work now.

"Where exactly are we going?" she asked, her voice more breathless than she wanted it to be.

"Here." Blade stopped before a partially closed door and pushed it open with his shoulder.

Blade didn't halt until he'd tugged her before a teak table with a single globe sitting on its surface. "Here. This is it."

It looked like her father's study at home—book-lined walls, leather chairs, Persian rugs quieting one's footsteps. It took several very erratic heartbeats for Vaughn to register that it was empty.

He released her arm only to raise his hand reverently to skim the curve of the high-relief globe. A lover's caress, reminding her very much of the previous night.

Keep focused, Vaughn, you're not out of trouble yet.

She waited, letting her pulse slow, her mind formulate and discard theories.

When Blade spoke again, he was no longer looking at her but staring at the globe as if it held the secrets of the universe.

"When I was a child," he said, "my father had a globe much like this. Though nothing so grand." He glanced up with a wistful smile. "In the evenings, he would talk to me of history. Of kingdoms conquered. Of magical places whose names are no more."

He sounded so lost Vaughn wanted to reach out and somehow soothe him. But there was a key here. A key she might be able to use to save his life, or her own, if she understood what it was.

"He told me of czars, of kings and princes. Men who created and defined their worlds."

Was this it, then? Was this what was driving him to auction a lethal weapon to the highest bidder?

"He told me that such men made their own rules. They lived by them and died by them."

His voice slid away.

She swallowed and stepped closer, watching his fingers sketch the crumbling boundaries of his own changing homeland.

"Is this why you're having this auction?" she asked, barely holding her breath.

He did not answer her directly but shook his head and said, "You know what it is like to live in the shadow of one's father. We always had this in common."

"Yes."

"Only yours is very much alive and mine is not."

Now she was only getting confused. Was he doing this to prove something to his late father? Or to himself?

"Blade, I don't understand." She watched his gaze shift from the globe to her face. Walking amidst land mines came to mind as she groped for the right words. "But if it helps, I've learned that we can't live for our fathers, only for ourselves. Our choices, our mistakes, our lessons are just that—ours. Not theirs."

"Are they?"

"Yes, I think—"

A commotion behind the closed door stopped her words.

She heard a thud and an oath, and then the door slammed open, revealing Stone standing there, looking typically calm and rocklike, and a slightly doubled-over guard groaning.

The mood in the room quickly changed. Blade stepped away from the globe, nodding at a trio of guards who'd materialized behind Stone.

"That is enough."

They grunted and disappeared, taking their limping comrade with them.

Stone never glanced Blade's way. Instead his intense gaze zeroed in on her with the old you've-screwed-things-up-again look.

Vaughn shook her head, an automatic movement one could construe as a very wifely gesture when dealing with an impossible man. Her next comment cemented her role. "Darling, whatever is the problem?"

She stepped toward him, her hands fisted at her side to keep from clobbering him. She'd been that close to getting Blade to open up to her. A step she needed to stop the auction before it ever began. But the opportunity was now lost.

"You forgot?" Stone's tone held even, until he looked at Blade. "Wives," he added, shrugging. "They're enough to make a man crazy."

Her sentiments exactly. Only not about wives—about husbands.

Blade grinned, no doubt part of a male bonding thing. It was tempting to slap both of them.

"Forgive me for dominating your wife's time. It is inexcusable."

"Vaughn, dear." Stone spoke again. "You forgot you

were to meet me before the auction. Which I do believe should be starting any moment."

No, slapping was too easy. Way too painless.

"Of course I haven't forgotten the auction."

Keep it light. No matter what.

She turned to Blade. "I'm excited about it."

"This is good. You shall be pleased." His tone sounded like a patriarchal Russian czar, but at least he wasn't asking pointed questions about Stone's forceful entry. Or why.

"Why don't we proceed to the main hall now?" Blade gestured with his hand that they should lead the way.

"In a moment." Vaughn offered a very tight smile. "I need to talk to—to my husband, for just a moment."

Male glares were exchanged before Blade nodded, gave her a half bow and walked regally from the room.

Vaughn waited until the door closed behind him before she stepped close enough to Stone so her whispered words could only be heard one-on-one.

"Of all the stupid—"

"Your transmitter went dead." His words were grating.

"I turned it off."

She read the shock in his eyes, then felt the force of his grip on her arm. "You what?"

"Turned it off. It was a private conversation."

"There's nothing private about this. Play reunion on your own time. He's the target."

"No, he's not." Could she make him understand, or

was she saying that more for her own benefit? "I was this close to finding out why he was auctioning whatever he's auctioning."

"We're not here for that."

He may not have been, but she couldn't walk away from a friend in need.

"I was getting the intel," she said.

"You were cozying up to a killer."

As if she hadn't slept with one last night? She held her tongue, but Stone obviously registered her thoughts as he stepped closer, close enough to brush up against her.

Her breath hitched as his words reached her.

"Do not confuse last night with the mission."

What the hell did that mean?

"Believe me, I haven't." She bit her upper lip. "It was a mistake and won't happen again." She was lying through her teeth.

"Dream on, deb."

How had they gotten so far off track? They were not the mission—Blade, or, more importantly, whatever Blade was auctioning, was the mission. It was time to remember that.

She shifted, snapping her mind back to the primary issue at hand and ignoring the promise in Stone's eyes.

"Blade said there would be two auctions. A primary one here, a secondary one with only the high bidders later."

"He say why?" Stone the agent was back. Thank heavens.

"Security reasons."

"Not good." He repeated her thoughts verbatim and she hadn't even told him about her father's people prowling about. "It most likely means the item being auctioned isn't on the premises. Which makes sense."

"But why go to all the effort to get everyone here?" she asked.

"Vetting the serious players." He gave a wolf's grin. "Very strategic. Also the top bidders, once they know the prize, will have to make payment arrangements, et cetera. They'll have a better idea of how much and how soon they'll need to pay for their new toy or toys. My guess is Blade will give them twenty-four, maybe forty-eight hours to make final payment arrangements."

"That's good news for us." She was seeing where Stone was going with his analysis.

He looked at her then, no longer man to woman but agent to agent. "We just got ourselves a larger window of opportunity."

"To what? We'll already know what's being auctioned. Isn't that what we're here for?"

"Plans have changed, princess."

Again? That did not sound good. On the other hand, her adrenaline was already kicking in. She arched one eyebrow, a move her mother would have recognized.

He answered, "That's right. New objective is to neutralize or retrieve the said weapon."

"Neutralize? As in destroy?"

"If necessary."

"And Blade?"

He looked at her, really looked, his expression blank before he doled out carefully measured words. "The orders are the same."

"We're to kill Blade."

"If necessary."

Chapter 18

Vaughn and Stone met Blade in the large foyer of the hotel as guests mingled and jockeyed on their way toward the main hall where the auction was to be held. Several guards clustered near Blade, gesturing toward the drive leading to the hotel.

Blade shot her a cautious, wary look before it was replaced with his normal charming expression. "Ah, you have arrived," he said, a little too forcefully.

As if there had been any doubt. Vaughn glanced out the hotel's front windows, noticing three men flanking a fourth. A tourist, judging by the travel-rumpled khaki outfit he wore and the camera slung around his neck.

Wind whipped around the men, kicking up dust and small pieces of debris.

"Problem?" Stone asked, beating her to the punch.

"Paparazzi." Blade looked only at her.

"Not my friends." She raised her hands in mock surrender.

Blade said nothing but inclined his head toward the reception room beyond him. "Shall we enter?"

This time, she and Stone led.

The hall was packed as she walked with Stone to the semicircular space open near the front. Every seat was filled; Blade waved her and Stone to two places in front. A wide set of windows beyond him showed the coming storm darkening the sky.

Blade strode to the center of the stage, as Vaughn slid onto a chair and not a moment too soon. She waited for her stomach to settle and her knees to stop quaking. It reminded her of her first piano recital, in Paris, at the embassy, with dignitaries from around the world politely eyeing her. Not a friendly face in the crowd. Then she'd thrown up twice before she wobbled to her seat, never so thankful as when she could turn her back on everyone and pretend they were not there.

Today she didn't have that option. She fiddled with her watch, hoping her team could pick up every word of the auction and that the storm brewing outside didn't affect communication.

"Gentlemen, and lady." Blade looked directly at her and nodded. "Thank you for your interest. If you'll look at your computer screens, we'll begin the auction."

Someone had slid a slim computer onto her lap. Vaughn glanced at the blue screen, not knowing what would happen next.

There was an air of hushed expectancy in the room. Vaughn felt the adrenaline rush one had before stepping out of a plane for the first parachute jump, the first bungee jump, the thrust of first sex.

She glanced around, noting the beaded sweat on foreheads and the gazes focused intently on laptop screens; one man was rolling his prayer beads.

Next to her, Stone, the consummate professional, remained calm. She wondered how many missions it would take for her to learn to be so detached. Then she smiled. A big assumption there—multiple missions. That wasn't going to happen if she and Stone didn't survive this one.

Now, there was an interesting thought. She and Stone—not lovers, but partners. It seemed so natural, like breathing air. No longer adversaries, but partners.

Blade cleared his throat and she glanced up.

His voice washed over the crowd, very precise, very clear, with only a hint of his motherland.

"You'll see on your screens the specs for the single item up for bid today. But before you begin, I will let you know that only today's top five bidders will be allowed into the final bidding round."

Up the ante. Increase the tension. And the competition. Stone was right. A very strategic move.

"A little background." Blade's tone surged with pride. "Less than ten years ago, Russia launched an experimental, modified communications satellite. Like so much else in the new Russian economy, one has become available for sale."

The unspoken term—spy satellite—whipped silently through the room.

"This satellite is run by a plutonium core."

Even without a science degree, Vaughn understood the implications. Plutonium meant a nuclear weapon.

The stakes had just escalated, big-time.

What was Blade planning?

"In addition to the preprogrammed controls, this particular satellite has advanced attitude control rockets."

"Sacre bleu," a man whispered in the front row.

She glanced his way, noting the way his eyes opened wide, how his chin trembled. Maybe she should have studied her physics harder. What did the addition of rockets mean?

Blade answered as if her unspoken question had been asked aloud. "Which means that activation of these rockets will allow the satellite to be brought down on any specific location in the world."

Now she got it.

"Washington, D.C. Jerusalem. Beijing. The possibilities are limited only by one's imagination and nerve."

Instant death for anyone in its path.

Her stomach plummeted. This was not her Blade. Her friend. The man who once saved her skin.

This man was selling the possibility of annihilating millions of innocents in one direct attack.

He couldn't possibly…

She glanced around the room, watching greed and power materialize before her eyes. The individual, group or country that controlled that satellite would be a force to be reckoned with.

Blade smiled at her, as if translating her shocked silence for approval.

How could he? How could she sit there and listen?

Stone nudged her arm and she dropped her gaze. Not that anyone but a blind man would be unable to read the horror, the disgust ripping through her.

Stone's words came back to her. *Neutralize and eliminate the weapon. Neutralize and eliminate Blade.*

There could be no reasonable explanation for what he was doing. This wasn't father love driving him. This was something else. He'd been wrong when he'd spoken to her earlier; they were nothing alike. Nothing.

Blade glanced around the room, raising one hand before continuing. "The one stipulation on the auction is that once the bidder has been given the attitude control and its codes, they will have thirty days to activate them. At the end of thirty days, the satellite has been preprogrammed to re-enter Earth's orbit, harmlessly disintegrating in the process."

Thirty days. Was that good news or bad? It might be a window of opportunity to stop mass murder, but not if the control mechanism and codes passed out of Blade's hands and into those of a terrorist organization before they were stopped. Was the team hearing this?

Ling Mai must have foreseen this. But not the magnitude of the task. This wasn't a stinger missile or even an extra-large order of the plastic explosive Semtex. This weapon could change the world forever.

Blade, what are you doing?

Blade raised his hands behind the podium and pointed to a digital reader board. "Bids, though not bidders, will be displayed automatically on the above board. Remember, only the top five bidders will be allowed to compete in the final auction with today's last bid starting the next round. If we're ready—" he looked around the crowd, smiled and nodded "—then we'll start the bidding at one hundred million."

A buzz whipped around the room as fingers clicked on keyboards, and the red-eyed numbers on the reader board danced before her.

Her own limbs froze, unable to move, unable to do anything but grip the laptop with trembling hands.

"One hundred fifty million. Do I see more?"

What if he succeeded? How many millions would die?

Voices in several languages ebbed and flowed, growing louder, but not enough to drown out Blade's voice.

"Five hundred ten million. Five hundred ten million to hold the world hostage."

She leaned forward in her chair, a voyeur at the feeding frenzy around her. Helpless to do anything but wait. Bile gagged her.

"Eight hundred million."

Blade turned toward her, but she kept her gaze straight ahead, not trusting him to see anything but shock and horror in her expression.

"Three billion."

"Three billion once."

Blade's face was lit from a fire within, his voice ablaze.

"Three billion twice."

"Three billion three times." Strained silence. "The auction is closed."

She rose, hearing the mayhem around her, a riot of sound and voices swelling, tensions teetering on razor edges. Her knees trembled, but she had to move, to get away. It wasn't fear propelling her, but the gut-deep knowledge that any second she was going to be sick.

Who was she to think she was ready to play hardball in this world? God, what a joke. She'd thought she was jaded, but *this,* this left her reeling. Ling Mai was wrong; Vaughn didn't belong here. Vaughn was wrong, too; she was so not cut out for this role.

"Pull it together," Stone whispered at her side.

Like a physical slap she heard her mother's voice.

Behave yourself, Vaughn. This reception is important.

You know how to greet the representative from Senegal, or Myanmar, or Burundi, Vaughn. Don't embarrass us.

You've been taught the right way, Vaughn. And don't forget it.

In the space between overwhelming horror and her body crying out to flee, she turned, her mother's smile in place, her training leading when all else failed.

She was not *invisible,* she was Vaughn Monroe Werner. Daughter of an ex-ambassador. Trained to function properly regardless of personal emotions. Schooled in correct behavior. Bastion of the public persona.

She had been chosen for this mission for a reason. And the reason wasn't to run when the going got rough. Stone's training might have taught her how to physically survive, but her upbringing was needed now.

Her gaze settled on Blade, even though she was all too aware of Stone standing to her left, his gaze no doubt searching for more signs of implosion from her.

Blade still stood in the center of the room, his grin growing larger, his chest rising and falling as if finishing a fast race. He glanced over at her and she nodded. Let him translate that any way he wanted.

Millions could die and he gloated.

Vaughn was thankful she'd eaten nothing so far that day; her stomach would not have been able to hold it.

And then Blade was beside her, his voice very Russian, his hand outstretched to grasp her own. "Well, Vaughn, what do you think?"

That you've lost it. Are certifiably insane. That there had to be an explanation to reconcile this man with her image of the Blade she knew, or once had known.

She waved her free hand, buying precious seconds to erase all censure from her voice. "I think you've surprised me."

His expression tightened, as did his grip. "I told you we've changed, both you and me. We've grown up, no?"

"We have changed." *But not this much.* Or was her Blade only a facade? Just as she had been. Playing by the rules of one's peers, hiding one's true self. But Blade a mass murderer?

Fortunately she wasn't required to say more as he turned toward Stone.

"Mister Stone." Blade's voice was neutral, nothing like the exaltation of seconds ago. His hand dropped from Vaughn's. "Congratulations."

She glanced between the two men's predatory grins. It was a little like being the only guppy in a bowl of hungry piranhas.

Blade's voice sounded very Russian as he responded to her confusion. "Your husband has won. He is one of our five finalists."

"You're right, darling." Stone wrapped one arm around Vaughn's waist. "These auctions are fun. And so stimulating."

If she hadn't been raised by a diplomat and his wife, wasn't in a public venue *and* undercover, she'd have thrown her hands up and walked away.

In a heartbeat.

Fortunately that option was taken away when one of the winning bidders approached Blade.

The Russian turned to speak to the man as Vaughn gathered her shattered composure.

Now what? Stone had won. At least one of them had kept their cool long enough to find a way into the final auction, and it hadn't been her.

"Vaughn?"

She wasn't even aware Blade had returned to her side and was talking to her until he nudged her arm.

"Is there a problem?" he asked, a frown darkening his expression.

What could possibly be wrong? A bomb capable of killing millions about to be passed into the hands of killers. A friend she no longer recognized. A direct order to stop the unstoppable but with no idea how.

And to think that only a few months ago, her biggest worries involved choosing which outfit to wear to a celebrity event.

"No, nothing's wrong." She gave what she hoped was a convincing smile; it was hard to tell with her facial muscles frozen. "I was just wondering, what happens now?" She glanced around those still milling in the room. "What if one of the unlucky bidders decides to take things into his own hands by kidnapping you to get the control and codes?"

Blade laughed. "There is no worry. The control is not at the hotel and without it, the codes mean nothing."

One issue clarified. A move on Blade could not be made until she and Stone located the control device. Her guess was that if something did happen to Blade, another could step in, retrieve the device and proceed to sell it to the highest bidder at a later date. There might even be a second set of the codes as a backup.

"What now, then?" she asked in all sincerity.

"I have a private jet waiting to take all the winners to the location of the final auction. No one will know the destination until we are in the air."

"Fine." She trusted herself to glance at Stone, who remained silent at her side, letting her extract intel in the way she'd been trained. But not by him. By her up-bringing. It was why Ling Mai had chosen her. "I'll go upstairs and pack my bags."

"No need to, my dear." Blade spoke to her, but kept his gaze on Stone. "I've had my people do that for you."

Alarm bells jangled internally, or maybe it was the pressure of Stone's arm around her waist tightening.

"Fine, then." *Play pretty, Vaughn. Don't let them see you sweat.* "Then I guess we're ready."

"We want to leave before the storm strikes." Blade nodded to someone behind her and added, "In my personal car, Vassily. Vaughn and her husband only. See to the rest of the guests also."

Blade walked away, far enough for her to lean against Stone and whisper in his ear.

"Bad news or good?"

"The rushed departure?"

No, the weather forecast.

Play nice, Vaughn. Remember, Stone is on your side, most of the time.

"Yes, the travel arrangements."

"Not sure."

Why couldn't he have lied to her and reassured her? But then again, this was Stone.

She glanced at her watch. "You think they know?" she asked Stone as he started to move away.

He shrugged.

Men. Next time, she was going to ask for Jayleen as a partner. Unsettling tarot cards aside, at least the woman spoke in full sentences.

Stone turned to look at her. "You coming?"

"Right behind you, darling."

She just hoped it wasn't a decision she was going to regret.

Chapter 19

Some days simply went to hell faster than others. Vaughn was trapped in one of them. Staring out into the teeming mass of humanity that was India from Blade's limousine, she tried to tune out everything around her and focus on a plan. Any plan. But nothing materialized.

The limo, large enough for eighteen passengers, cramped her, made her feel as if she were in a gilded cage. It contained only Blade, three of his security guards, herself and Stone, and one very silent, very distant driver. She'd watched the other auction winners, some dressed in Armani and others in poor ill-tailored knockoffs pile into two other limos, their expressions a mixture of triumph and wariness. Not that she blamed them. Only one would walk away the final winner, with the power to annihilate.

Her stomach twisted.

"You look pensive," Blade remarked, lolling against the leather seat across from her.

"Just curious about where we're heading." She reached for some bottled water, chilled and ready at hand.

"And I always thought of you as being open to surprises," Blade said with a laugh.

"Surprises, yes." She sipped to wet her dry throat. *Think before you speak,* she warned herself. *For once, think before you speak.* "And you have surprised me."

"With the auction?" He leaned forward, his hands clasped across his knees, looking so much like the old Blade—fun, flirtatious, always up for a new experience. What had happened? Had he changed or had she? And how did she stop him from going any farther down this dangerous path?

"Yes." She, too, leaned forward, aware of Stone silent at her side, aware of the risk she was about to take. "Why, Blade?"

He looked momentarily perplexed until he sat back and laughed, the sound vibrating around the inside of the car like a tidal wave.

"Ah, Vaughn." He wiped his eyes and glanced at Stone. "Your wife, she is still so, so—"

"Naive?" came Stone's laconic reply.

"Yes. A good word." Blade stopped laughing and said something in Russian to the driver. "Vaughn is still so naive, and innocent, are you not?"

Vaughn wasn't sure she liked being the butt of these two men's comments. But it wasn't the words alone that worried her; it was Blade's tone. Something was up.

She glanced out the window, aware they had been traveling west, back into Simla's crescent-shaped ridge, but instead of heading directly west toward the main road to Delhi, their car had veered off and was now heading north, winding along steep narrow streets jammed with native bazaars and verandah-like sidewalks. They were no longer traveling toward Delhi, nor were they traveling with the other two limos.

Something was definitely up and she didn't like it.

A quick glance at Blade revealed a curious shuttered expression, much like a hawk watching a trapped mouse. Stone tensed at her side. He might not have been familiar with the terrain, but no doubt picked up on the silent tension now whipping through the vehicle.

"What's going on, Blade?" she demanded. Let him think her naive, but she was still a diplomat's daughter and understood the value of timing. Now was not the time to be cowed or meek. "Where exactly are we going?"

"You'll see when we get there."

It was not a good answer.

Stone shifted in his seat and three weapons were immediately drawn and aimed. At him and at her.

"You treat all your guests this way?" Stone said, sitting back very, very slowly, both his hands in plain sight and relaxed before him.

Blade didn't answer him but spoke to her. "How is your father, Vaughn? We have not really discussed him."

When in doubt, bluff. "Last I spoke to him he was fine. Why?"

The smile curving Blade's lips did nothing to settle her stomach. "He is aware of your marriage?"

This time, she was the one who laughed, though it came out as more of a strangled wheeze. "Very much aware." Then, because there wasn't much to lose, she added, "Aware and unhappy. You still haven't told me why you're asking about him or—" she glanced at the weapons still held high "—or why we're playing this silly game."

"Ah, but Vaughn, life is all a game." He glanced again at Stone. "I'm sure your husband here would agree."

Stone nodded but remained quiet.

"Look." Patience never was her strong suit. So let him see what he expected to see. "Stop with the cryptic comments, the threats." She waved one hand toward the closest thug and heard everyone inhale as the man jerked the gun slightly higher. She ignored them all. "And tell me what's going on. Is this because Stone won at the auction? Or does it have something to do with my father?"

The car slowed before Blade answered. It slowed and pulled between two peeling stucco buildings, almost scraping against the walls. Darkness closed in as overhanging balconies and the incoming rain clouds blocked the afternoon light.

The lane took only a moment to pass through and beyond, but Vaughn could have sworn it took years.

They had emerged into a wide field, dotted with hundreds of blood red poppies, incandescent against the dark low-lying clouds nearly kissing the ground.

Vaughn's heart sped up as the car halted and the motor stilled.

The nearest goon glanced once at Blade before opening his door and stepping out, gun still plainly visible. Another thug waved Vaughn and Stone forward, his weapon giving them few options except to comply.

Only when she emerged into the muggy, thick air did Vaughn realize how chilly she felt. Only Stone at her backside kept her from shivering. No doubt such a move would earn a black mark in her already crowded copybook.

A quick glance around gave her few clues as to their location, but did alert her to one pertinent fact. The sight of a modified Mi-8 turbo engine Russian helicopter.

Was this good news or bad?

She turned to Blade, who was just then exiting the car. "Is this some kind of joke? A game to see if you can scare your guests before you fly them to the next auction?"

"No."

Okay, that answered one question. This was bad news.

"Then what's going on?" She fisted her hands on her hips. Let Blade believe it was from outrage; in truth, it was to keep them from shaking.

His gaze was level and steady as he spoke. "The man outside the hotel earlier."

She shook her head, wondering where the conversation was heading now. "What man?"

"One of the paparazzi."

She'd forgotten all about him. The auction of a weapon of mass destruction tended to push small details to the back of one's memory. Her voice held honest confusion. "What about him?"

"I believe your father sent him."

The penny dropped with a sickening thud.

"My father sent a—no wait, you're saying the man wasn't one of the paparazzi but a CIA agent?" Alex's words came back to haunt her. Not that she was about to let Blade know that. Instead she stepped forward, waving her hands before her. "Are you kidding? My father is the director of Central Intelligence. These are not his servants to be ordered around at a whim." She glanced pointedly at Blade's own guards. "So you jumped to the erroneous conclusion that CIA agents are following me around India, on my honeymoon, to what? Take photos of my new husband? I'm sure Father has plenty without extras. What's really going on here, Blade?"

"You tell me."

"Tell you what?"

"Was that man following you or with you?"

Her voice rose. "You can't possibly be saying what I think you're saying." She was taking a few lessons from her sister. Chrissie in a snit was a sight to behold. "First I'm naive." She glared at Stone, including him in her fit of pique. "Then my father is having me trailed, and now." She threw her arms in the air. A risky move with jumpy men holding loaded weapons. "And now you're accusing me of being a spy? A secret agent. That, that has to be the best joke of all. Isn't it, Stone?"

Her pseudo-husband gave her a wide grin.

Her outrage, only partially faked, seemed to turn the tide, as Blade shook his head and stepped closer to her, raising one hand to lay it gently against her cheek. A gesture she remembered from days gone by. A connection.

"Vaughn, I cannot take the risk," he said, his eyes darkening. "I wish to believe you are still innocent. For old times' sake."

She felt the warmth of his hand, the thick air swirling around her as the advancing storm gained ground, heard the slow wind of the helicopter warming up its engines. It was all so surreal. Until Stone cleared his throat and the present slammed against her.

"So what?" she asked, her voice subdued. "What are you going to do with us?" *Are we dead?*

Blade shook his head, answering her unspoken question first. "I shall leave you two here. My gift to you. *Ciao, bella.* If I thought you were in truth an agent, you would be dead."

Then he turned to walk away, taking all three guards with him.

Vaughn didn't know if she wanted to shout and run after him, or flee just as fast in the other direction. Instead she did nothing. Stood stock-still while he clambered aboard the helicopter, its blades kicking up dust and wind. He glanced at her once, raising a hand in farewell, and the chopper rose then flitted off like a dragonfly toward the west.

"Damn," Stone whispered beside her.

She wasn't sure if it was relief or frustration behind his single word.

Behind her the limo's engine roared to life. The driver speedily fishtailed back down the small alleyway.

She and Stone were alone. Alive, but as effectively neutralized as if they'd been hog-tied and gagged back at the hotel.

Stone's voice broke through to her. "Communication with the team is out. The storm, or location, or both, is interfering with the commsets."

Great. The day was just getting better and better.

"You going to do something here or just play mannequin?" Stone asked her.

"Yeah, I'm going to do something." Anger was slowly replacing the fear of only moments ago. A fear based on knowing that any second her life could end.

But it hadn't, and she still had a job to do.

She slung her Prada bag off her shoulder, glad Blade's goons had thought to retrieve it from her room and give it to her before they'd entered the limo. Her hand closed over her cell phone.

"You've got to be kidding," Stone said at her side, frustration replacing his earlier tone.

"No." She racked her memory for a number and flipped open the pink, rhinestone-studded clamshell case. Punching in the number, she looked at Stone. "I may be naive, but I am not without resources. Why don't you make yourself useful. Run down that alleyway and find us a cab."

"To do what?" he asked, spearing one hand through his hair. "In case you haven't noticed, we are in the middle of nowhere, your boyfriend just choppered out of here to attend a second auction in a secret location and even if we knew where it was being held, we have no way of getting there."

"Oh ye of little faith." A singsong voice answered on the other end of the line and she focused on it. "Is this the Fagu Potato Research Center? Good. May I speak to Wilfred Huntington III?"

"What—" Stone sputtered. A very un-Stone-like sound.

"Trust me," she told him. "Find the taxi. We'll be on our way in less than thirty minutes and arrive at Blade's auction location a good three to four hours ahead of him."

"How?"

"Trust me."

Chapter 20

"What the—"

"It seats two." Vaughn headed toward the plane at a fast clip; they'd already lost twenty-three minutes and the clock was ticking.

"Looks like a T-38 Talon."

"It isn't."

"Then what—cripes, it's a Javelin."

Should have figured Stone would know about the newest private jet available to billionaires with the need for prestige and power beneath their fingertips.

"It's not even on the market yet," he whispered, scanning the thirty-five-foot length of gleaming aluminum. "How the hell are you going to fly it?"

"Don't worry, big boy. I'm rated for multiengine instrument flying and have the required turbine hours I need."

"Vaughn." He stood his ground. Rock man was back. "This is a prototype. Not even on the market. You can't hop in and drive it like the family car."

She glanced at the plane. "In most cases, you'd be right."

There. That was it for being understanding. They didn't have time to review her qualifications. Or lack of them, which he didn't have to know. She was his only chance to get them both to where Blade most likely was. End of story.

"So what does this have to do with a Potato Research Center?"

She circled the outside, doing a preflight inventory before returning to his side. "I have this friend—"

"Should have figured."

"—who took me for a spin or two in this puppy a while back. He also happens to be very involved in different aspects of sustainable agriculture. He also owns half of Idaho—or is it Montana? Anyway, I took a chance he'd be at the Research Center and came in on this."

"Big risk." Stone didn't sound impressed, especially when he added, "How long ago?"

"Oh, he arrived about a week—"

"Vaughn."

Not a good sign when he used her real name.

"Doesn't matter. Either we get in this and fly it out of here, possibly dying in the process, or we stand here and let Blade get away with killing who knows how many innocents. Your choice."

"First." He raised a finger of his right hand. "We don't even know where Golumokoff went. Second, even if we did, it's not likely the two of us can get past his security measures. And three, with communications still out we don't even have the team backing us. Then there's four." He glanced over his shoulder at the storm clouds pressing closer every minute. "Four, I'm not so sure it's safe to fly an experimental aircraft out of some makeshift airfield, through the Himalayas, with the mother of all storms rolling in."

"Chicken." She smiled at him, brushing aside a lock of hair that had blown across her face.

He shook his head, then released a belly laugh. "Hell, princess. Your old man screwed up big-time when he didn't nab you for the Agency."

Leave it to Stone to stop her in her tracks.

He was climbing into the plane when he turned around. "You might want to get a move on here."

That was almost a request.

It took her another three minutes to finish her preflight checklist and clamber into the cockpit. Fortunately, the Javelin had a hands-on throttle and stick and switch configuration that would make an instrument takeoff pretty straightforward if need be.

"Hold on to your hat, Stone."

There was no response, just a quick thumbs-up.

It wasn't glamorous. Or smooth. But she got them

into the air with only a few words her mother wouldn't have approved of.

At any other time, she would have avoided the Javelin's 49,000-foot ceiling and 528-knot cruising speed, but this time she couldn't afford to. She had one guess, and one guess only, to make the right call. And one chance to stop Blade. She had to get where he was headed before he did and to do so would require flying high above the commercial jet speed and ceiling.

"You keep trying to reach the team," she directed Stone over the headset. "See if they can meet us where we're going."

Though by the time they arrived all the fireworks should be over.

"And exactly where is it we're heading?"

It said something that he hadn't called her on this until now. Partners? Or did he finally trust her to lead as well as work in tandem?

"Italy," she replied. "Lake Como. Ling Mai should have the coordinates to Blade's house there."

"Any reason Italy?" Stone shot back.

Two small reasons. So small Stone had every right to call her insane for trusting so much to so little intel. The first was the phrase Blade used back in his hotel room when she'd been hiding behind a curtain. A phrase that included the words *Lake Como*. And the second hint, his parting phrase to the both of them. *Ciao, bella.* Goodbye, beautiful. Such a common expression, especially if one was already in an Italian mind-set.

But was that enough to tell Stone? Or would he shoot her down?

"Vaughn?" His voice nudged her.

"It's a gut feeling. You've got to trust me on this one."

He didn't reply.

So she added, "And see if you can have Ling Mai reach some of my father's people. No telling how much firepower Blade will have around the place. Stopping the transfer of the control and the password is too important to leave it just to us."

"Copy."

Another first. Stone taking orders that no doubt galled him as they did her. But she was right. This was no longer a test to see if Ling Mai's fledgling agency had the power to go where others could not. They'd already proved that. Now they had to have the experience to know when to call in the big guns. Even if such a call meant Vaughn and her father would face off head-to-head.

It wasn't a scenario Vaughn was looking forward to.

Calling Blade's home a house would be an understatement. It looked like the fourteenth-century palace it'd originally been. It had been built at a time when fortified accommodations were all the rage. Golden-toned stucco walls several feet thick surrounded an exterior courtyard; there were small windows on all the lower levels, and a solid wood door looked as if it ate battering rams for breakfast.

The trip from India to Milan's Malpensa Airport was

not as rough as it could have been. Some day, she'd tell Stone how little experience she really had with a Javelin. But not now.

Now the two of them were crouched on the private roadway leading to Blade's relatively secluded villa. The good news was it was obvious Blade had not arrived. The bad news was Vaughn might have guessed incorrectly.

"What now, princess?" Stone whispered at her side, adding, "If your boyfriend *is* coming, he could be here at any time."

"He's not my boyfriend and he will be here." She kept her gaze straight ahead, discarding one option after another as to how best get inside the villa. "My guess is Blade would have stashed both the control and passwords here before he left for India. Safer that way."

"We could scale the far wall, use the maneuvers we worked on first week at The Farm."

"Or we could try something else." She glanced over at what Stone was wearing and thought they just might be able to pull this off.

"I don't like that look, princess. What's your plan?"

"Simple." She grinned. "We go in by the front door."

Chapter 21

"This isn't a plan, it's suicide," Stone grumbled at her side, but he kept pace with her step by step as they approached the twelve-foot solid wood doors. Their footsteps crunched across the graveled drive. Close by several dogs barked, then subsided into low-pitched growls.

"Sure it's a plan." She glanced over at him, pausing long enough to ruffle his hair with one hand and earn a frown. "This is the Billy Bob and Angelina plan."

"The what?"

"You know? Billy Bob Thornton and Angelina Jolie arrived at some awards ceremony, disheveled, and Billy Bob says, 'We just bleeped in the limo on the way to the show.' You remember?"

He actually looked as if he had blushed. "My education is obviously lacking."

"Appalling." She grinned in spite of the rumba her stomach was doing because they'd reached the doors amid a rush of commotion on the other side of the stucco walls. She heard running footsteps, and dogs had started to bark.

She linked her arm with Stone's and grinned as if there were a dozen paparazzi snapping pictures as the door opened and a stern-faced young man faced them.

"Ciao," Vaughn gushed, adding a laugh when the man said nothing. *"Mi ciamo,* ah, oh." She glanced at Stone, who looked wooden, before she turned back to the man. "I'm sorry. I always mess up my Italian. I'm Vaughn Werner." She stuck out her hand, letting it dangle in empty space. She stepped closer to him, making sure she sounded deb-dim, aware Stone would cringe at the tone. "I'm an old friend of Blade's. Is he here?"

"No." The door started to close.

She stepped forward, tugging Stone with her. Two bodies made a better wedge than one. "But Blade told me to meet him here. Surely he should be arriving at any moment."

"No." The door shifted again, but it was blocked.

"Really." Vaughn fisted hands on her hips. "Find me a majordomo or head person. Someone I can speak with." When the man didn't move, she clapped her hands. Associating with the rich and famous had its advantages, and being able to act like an aristocratic pain in the backside was one of them.

The man nodded to someone behind the door. Seconds

ticked by while Vaughn held his gaze with an angled head. Soon the sound of heavy footfalls across marble floors reached her and a middle-aged woman who looked more like a peasant than majordomo moved into view.

"Thank heavens." Vaughn spoke to her directly. "A woman. These men know nothing."

"*Sì.*" The woman offered a faint smile, or maybe it was only a trick of the shadows.

"My name is Vaughn Werner and I'm a friend of Blade's. An old friend."

"*Sì.*"

So far, so good. At least they'd gotten around *no* as an only response.

She continued, "Last I saw Blade, he told me to meet him here. But this one—" she glanced at the first man still holding the door like a shield "—he doesn't know how to treat guests."

"Where you see *Signor* Blade?" the woman asked, suspicion darkening her eyes.

"In Simla. India. We were just there and flew directly in today." For good measure, she added, "Blade said he would be right behind us and that it would be perfectly fine to meet him at his villa." She threw up her hands in a gesture she'd seen her sister use with clerks and waiters. "But if it's too much of a problem, we'll just leave and you can deal with his wrath."

"No." The older woman stepped forward to peer at Stone. "And he?"

"I'm Billy Bob," came the drawled reply.

Vaughn bit back a groan. Just like Stone to manifest

a sense of humor at a time like this. She kept her smile firmly in place and focused on the woman before her.

"You may come in." The woman stepped back. "But wait only in the study of *Signor* Blade. Nowhere else."

Since the study was the most likely place Blade would have a safe, the idea was perfectly acceptable to Vaughn.

"Thank you." She frowned at the man slowly opening the door. "Obviously it's good to work with someone able to make command decisions."

Then the woman added, "The *signor* should be here at any time. He called from Milan and is coming."

Talk about bombs dropping.

Without saying more, tempting though it was, Vaughn and Stone followed the woman down a paneled hallway, their passage ringing off the Carrara marble floors. How long did they have? Thirty minutes? Less?

She gave the older woman a stiff smile as she closed the door behind them with a resounding click. It sounded awfully close to a death knell.

"Come on, Billy Bob," Vaughn whispered, scanning the art-lined walls and bookcases for the most likely place to cache a safe. The Jackson Pollock looked promising. But then so did the Miró.

Stone obviously didn't care for twentieth-century abstract painters as he was systematically checking the desk drawers.

To each his own.

Gently, in case there were booby traps or trip wires, Vaughn felt around the edges of both good-sized paintings. Nothing.

She tried a small Chagall and a watercolor by Winslow Homer.

Still nothing.

"You dusting or hunting for a wall safe?" Stone said from behind her.

"Don't get—" She turned and caught the faintest shadow along the far bookcase. Without another word she knelt beside the crack where molding met molding.

"In case you forgot the woman with one eyebrow, we don't have a lot of time—"

"Shh," she whispered, leaning closer to the case, catching the whiff of old leather bindings and dust. And something else. Something cool, damp and smelling of age.

It took breaking off two fingernails before Stone joined her and started searching, too.

"It's got to be here," she said, more to herself than him. "A lever or wheel or button. Something. There's a—"

And just like that, her elbow grazed a first edition Hemingway, *For Whom the Bell Tolls,* and the wall shifted on well-oiled hinges.

"Voilà." She grinned at Stone.

"Lucky guess."

"Jealous."

He grinned in reply as they faced a rough-hewn hardwood door that looked older than anything in the study. Older and more sinister. The hinges alone were thicker than Vaughn's forearm.

Instead of moving, though, Vaughn glanced around the room again. "I'm not so sure this is what we should be looking at. Given the cool air coming from beyond this door my guess is it leads to a cellar of some sort."

"Or a dungeon."

Stone, always the optimist.

"Yeah, or a dungeon. But I'd think Blade would have a safe here in this room. That's where he'd keep the controls and the codes. Not buried beneath the house."

"You always were very perceptive, my dear."

Vaughn froze, stealing a glance at Stone. The voice was not his.

It was Blade's.

Chapter 22

Vaughn stood silently beside the massive Louis XIV desk as two goons with guns disappeared behind the wooden door and down a series of stone-cut stairs into pitch darkness. Stone was sandwiched between the Russians like ham between Swiss cheese. He didn't even glance her way as the door swung shut behind them.

She smoothed damp palms along the front of her creased linen slacks—a little worse for wear given the excursions of the day.

"I am surprised to see you here." Blade strode to a humidor on a marble-and-glass side table. He plucked out a hand-rolled Cuban, slowly massaging it between his fingers as if they were discussing crossing paths on a Paris sidewalk. "Very surprised. CIA or another agency?"

"I told you I wasn't either."

"And your husband?"

"Get real." This next part bordered on the truth. "He's pissed. Getting dropped off in a field instead of being one of the bidders made him testy."

"So you came here because of your husband?"

"It was one of the reasons."

Blade remained quiet and Vaughn followed suit. No sense in provoking Blade in any way until she judged his tenor better. Right now, she'd guess somewhere between impressed and put out. Or maybe she was being a little optimistic.

"You have nothing more to say?" Blade lit his cigar and took a few deep, appreciative puffs.

She coughed instead. Not that she really minded cigar smoke in the right situation. But being in a small, enclosed room, with a Russian planning on selling death and destruction, with Stone as a hostage, was not the best of situations.

"It bothers you?" Blade asked, his eyes glowing like the amber cigar tip through the swirling smoke.

"What bothers me, Blade, is the thought of what you're about to do."

One eyebrow twitched.

In for a penny, in for a pound.

"I mean it." She stepped closer, fisting hands against her side. "You're about to hand over a weapon of mass destruction to some crazy terrorist who will kill hundreds of thousands, if not millions, to make some political point."

"You forgot for a tidy sum of money."

"This is not about the money and you know it."

"I do?" Now he sounded laconic.

"Of course it's not." She shook her head and added, "Not that I'm really sure what is driving you to do this idiotic thing."

"Idiotic? I hold your Stone at gunpoint and you call me an idiot?"

Ego alert. But this was Blade. They had a history together and, if she was going to stop him, she had to reach him, or that part of him she remembered.

"Look." She held his gaze steady. "It's not too late to stop all of this. Nothing has been done yet that is irrevocable."

Except for two dead MI6 agents, but take one step at a time.

"What is it you wish me to do?" he asked, puffing deeply. "Stop the auction now?"

"Yes. That's a great start."

"And the clients even now refreshing themselves after our journey? What do you propose I do with them?"

"What does it matter?" Her voice rose. There was a lot at stake here, and she wanted to get through to him. "They are nothing. Nobody to you. If they were in your place and had a chance to save their skin, they would in a heartbeat."

"Is this what you are doing, then? Saving my skin?"

"Yes." *Or at least trying.* "But I can't do it without your help. You must stop the auction and destroy the control and codes."

"And I will do this because?" His accent increased. "What do I get from these actions?"

"You'll live." She wanted to shake him. "Continue with the auction and you'll make the hunt for Osama Bin Laden pale in comparison."

"But I will make a name for myself then, no?"

"Is that what this is about?" *No. No. No.* "You're better than this. Bigger than this. Nothing, absolutely nothing good will come of continuing."

"I could kill your husband. That would bring a certain satisfaction."

A chill snaked through Vaughn, but she stifled it. It would only play into Blade's little game, whatever that was.

"This is not about Stone. Or me. It's about you. Your choice. Your last chance to walk away from a mistake so monumental it's hard to imagine."

"You have not answered me yet," he said, his voice thicker, deeper.

"Answered what?"

"What will I get for stopping now?"

"What is it you want?" She was practically shouting at him. Her mother would have been appalled. So would her father, but at least her father would have realized what hung in the balance and that any personal short-comings gave way to the greater good. "Tell me, and I'll see what I can do."

"You offer me you, then?" He smiled, but it wasn't warm.

"You don't want me." At least not the way he was implying. What was she missing here? "But I think there is something you want. What is it?"

"Ah, Vaughn, you are so—"

"Naive?"

"There is that." He walked around her to stand behind the desk. "And passionate. I do believe you care what happens to me."

"Of course I care. You saved my life once. I owe you."

"There is that."

"And you're my friend." At least she'd thought he was. Once. Lately the boundaries had become very murky.

But her words seemed to have reached him as he glanced away, for just a second, as if in internal debate. Then he glanced up.

She'd never seen such bleak, lonely eyes. Her heart twisted even as she squared her shoulders for what must come next. She'd lost. There'd be no going back.

"You're going to continue, aren't you?" she asked, fire no longer in her words.

"In my own fashion, yes."

"And nothing I can say will stop you?"

"No. Not now. It is too late."

"And what about Stone and myself?"

He pressed a buzzer on the desk. The far door swung open and the man she remembered from India stood there, his gaze fixed on his employer.

"Vassily, I would like you to escort our unexpected guest downstairs. She will be joining Marcos Stone."

Blade hadn't exactly said he was going to kill them, but what options did he have? He understood exactly where she stood and what she would do if released.

Checkmate.

"I'm sorry, Blade," she whispered, preparing to follow without a fight. Not here, at least.

"Sorry?"

"That it ends like this between us."

"You are so sure." He smiled then. A small, wistful expression she never would have associated with him.

But there was no time to ask what he'd meant by such a look or his cryptic statement. The solid wood door already yawned open, and Vassily did not look like the patient type.

"Goodbye, Blade," she murmured as she stepped on the first step.

If he answered, she never heard it.

Vassily accompanied her down, down, down, deep underneath the building. When they reached a level that must have at one time served as a cellar, or dungeon, they navigated a dark passageway lit only by the dimmest of bulbs. As they wound through the labyrinth, her sense of direction deserted her. The only thing that remained, besides fear, was the knowledge that she was heading toward Stone. And to think that less than a week ago, that would have been bad news.

Her Gucci flats slapped across the stone floor. The

good news was she hadn't chosen some snappy Kate
Spade or flirty Marc Jacobs strapless sandals earlier in the
day: they weren't exactly made for hightailing it out of
danger zones. Which was what she was in up to her
eyeballs.

Another thought for a future endeavor. If her career
as an agent bit the dust, maybe she could go into high-
fashion design for the woman who needed a little something extra—like a dress one could scale walls in,
handbags to hold weapons of a decent size or shoes
made to save one's neck and not break it. On second
thought, if she was no longer an agent, it would be
because she didn't make it through whatever Blade had
planned for her and Stone.

The devil is in the details, her father used to say. And,
as usual, he was right. She just hoped he wasn't right
about her getting in over her head with wanting to be a
member of the Agency.

But now wasn't the time to go there. Doubt did not
belong in a warrior's arsenal. She didn't know where
that pithy saying came from, but thought it deserved its
own needlework pillow. She'd commission one as soon
as she got out of this mess.

Yeah, like that was going to happen without help.
Like from her team, wherever they were.

As if she had summoned them, sounds erupted above
them. At first she thought it was champagne bottles
popping. Vassily looked down the empty hallway even
as he reached for a radio receiver on his belt.

He shouted into the speaker in Russian.

Vaughn froze, hearing more noises now, even from deep within the bowels of the house. Shouts outside the house, murmurs from somewhere above, a rat-a-tat-tat rippling close by. Russian voices roared in increasing crescendos.

Someone was attacking the villa. Her team? Or her father's people? Did it matter? The point was, now was her chance to make a break for it.

Taking tiny, incremental steps, partly because her legs felt like quaking aspens, she eased her way backward toward the wall. She pressed against it to give her the momentum she needed to execute phase one.

Taking Vassily down.

Chapter 23

With a move that would have made Stone proud, she launched herself from the wall straight into Vassily's sizeable girth, ramming him like a punching bag.

A quick pivot, turn and twist and she angled away from his grip.

He was faster than his size indicated.

But she'd had ballet and gymnastics training. Backflip, turn on point, foot up, heel to the jaw.

Vassily quivered and staggered back. But he wasn't down by any means.

What was that other lesson Stone had taught her? Street fighting. Down and dirty.

"Well, big boy," she panted, jockeying to a new stance. "I'm a quick study."

Not quick enough, she thought several moments later. Vassily was down on the floor, groaning and clutching his family jewels, but she'd wasted precious minutes as the sounds above and ahead grew stronger.

What next?

There were too many unknowns. Who was attacking the house and how would they be approaching it? Who made up the assault team—local *polizia?* Interpol? Her father's people? The list was endless, and daunting. Would they be on the lookout for her and Stone, or was it every man and woman for themselves? And what about Stone? If she managed to get to him, past the guard or guards, and liberate him, what then? Could they navigate the labyrinth of passageways to reach the main level?

Then there was the Stone versus Blade dilemma.

Should she save Stone and leave the satellite control to chance? She had come a long way since her first training days at The Farm in Maryland, but even she couldn't be in two places at the same time.

First things first. If she freed Stone, both of them could go after Blade and the codes; there was strength in numbers. Also, if she didn't save Stone and didn't make it out of this place alive, who would even know he was held hostage down here? No one, most likely.

Stone first. Blade second.

She dashed straight ahead, only too aware that flat soles on stone floors did not take corners well. No wonder the pros preferred crepe; it kept one from falling on her pride. For a second, the sound of a second pair of shoes running behind her reached her. Then stopped.

She didn't have time to investigate.

"You're losing it," she hummed to herself, rocketing down a set of stairs. "Let's hope this is the right direction."

Up ahead she spied what had to be her goal—Stone's cell. One of Blade's men, holding a semiautomatic weapon, guarded a closed door.

Now what?

She continued to move toward him, a little slower now, catching her breath and aware of each move he made—the near silent turn toward her as he noticed her, the shifting of gun from barrel to ceiling to barrel straight at her, the tensing of his muscles.

This guy was primed to fight.

"Blade," she gasped, stumbling as she drew within twenty feet of the man. "Blade has been shot." She pointed in the direction of where she'd just come. "Up there. In the study. Hurry. He needs help. He's alone."

She thanked the gods he understood at least a little English as his frown turned darker.

"Hurry," she shouted, waving her hands in the agitated manner she'd learned from a fifth-grade English teacher who later had been taken away for a long rest. "He needs help."

"I hear nothing." The man tapped his headset.

Damn, she'd forgotten about that.

"No one knows. We were alone." She spread her own hands before her. "I have no radio. No weapon.

They came from the front hallway. Blade killed one and was shot. Oh, God, you've got to help him!"

Her words—or, more likely, her desperation—got through to him as he glanced at the door.

"You stay here." He motioned with his weapon to the hallway. "No go anywhere."

"Don't worry." She sagged against the nearest wall. "I'm not going anywhere."

So, it was only a little lie. In the grand scheme of what was happening it barely counted.

The man gave a grunt and shot down the hallway, lumbering past her with a determination that would make a rhino proud.

She waited till she heard his footfalls turn the corner before she rushed through the door.

Her picklock-cum-necklace trembled in her hand as she searched for the best pick to use, aware of every precious passing second.

At last she found the right size and inserted it into the lock, listening as much as she could for the click and tumble.

"Hurry. Hurry. Hurry." It became a mantra. Had the guard realized yet he'd been duped? Was there another guard on the other side of the door? What was happening upstairs? "Focus, Vaughn. Focus."

With a last mighty twist, she felt the give of the lock. Rising in a quick motion she wished, not for the first time, that she had some type of weapon.

Too late now.

She pushed open the door, taking a deep breath, and

stepped into the room. Before she had moved more than a foot forward, an arm snagged her throat from behind.

She staggered backward, her air supply cut off. Fingers clawing an arm made of steel did nothing. Pinpricks of light danced before her.

"You're late," a male voice growled in her ear.

The pressure decreased.

She turned and slugged Stone. Not that it had much oomph, not nearly enough.

"You could have killed me." Massaging her bruised windpipe gave her a second to breathe.

"I didn't. What's the plan?"

That quick, Mister Take-Charge Stone was back.

"The plan is to get you out of here before Bruiser Boris comes back and brings friends."

"Who's coming through the front gates?"

"I don't know."

He gave her his patented you've-got-to-be-kidding look.

"What do you—"

"Look, in spite of what you think, I haven't been upstairs eating bonbons." She stepped away, getting a good look at him and shaking her head. He looked more than a little worse for wear. "Did they rough you up?"

"You wish," he snapped. Obviously captivity had not mellowed him one bit. He also hadn't answered her question.

"I mean, are you up to—"

"Lead the way, I'll be right behind."

Yeah, right. Even now he was holding one arm across his ribs.

She stepped closer, a little like moving toward an enraged lion in a cage when all your instincts shouted at you to flee. Not waiting for permission she positioned herself on his left side, preparing to slip beneath his arm to offer support.

"What the hell are—"

"We can argue or we can move it. I have no idea how much time we have, so I'd suggest shutting up and dealing with it."

"I don't need—"

"Sure you don't." She maneuvered herself beneath his arm and, as gingerly as possible given the time crunch and situation, wrapped her right hand around his waist. His sharp intake of breath told her how bad it was. "Let's move, Stone. I have a nail appointment I'm late for."

She thought he grinned. Or maybe it was a grimace, as they hobbled toward the door. She leaned him forward to glance down the hallway.

"Empty."

Good. That meant Boris was lost or delayed. Either option was good.

"Which way?" Stone inhaled deeply.

To the left meant back the way she came. She had no clue what lay to the right. She glanced in that direction and spied, down the long length, a form silhouetted in a partially open doorway. Blade?

"The controls should still be upstairs." Stone breathed heavily. "We'll need to—"

"No." She straightened slightly and heard Stone's moan. "I just saw Blade. To the right, through a doorway."

Stone shifted to look in the direction she indicated. Down the empty hallway, shielded in shadows now that the door had been closed.

"You sure?" he asked. Not that she blamed him. A brief glance, fueled by adrenaline, and no clear image, only an impression. They risked a lot if they started chasing a phantom.

"Blade would escape with the codes. The control is useless without it." Hadn't Stone told her that himself? Or maybe she was making it up. "I'm sure it was Blade leaving by that door."

"Where's it go to?"

"I don't know."

Tension radiated from his body. Tension and energy draining as he weighed the options.

"It was Blade, I know—"

"I believe you."

Slap her with a two-by-four. "You do?"

"Of course I do. The question is, can we stop him?"

So maybe Stone had changed over the last days, just as she had. A week ago, she didn't think he had the word *we* in his vocabulary. Or that he'd let her take the lead. But she was and it was decision time.

"Let's—" But she couldn't finish, not when a growl alerted the two of them that they were no longer alone in the hallway. Bruiser Boris was back, with a buddy right behind him. One glance at his face revealed he was none too happy.

Chapter 24

Stone shifted until they both pivoted to face the guards, still a good fifteen feet away. Both had guns, and she and Stone were locked together like a bad circus act.

Until Stone dropped his arm and separated the two of them.

He was the one hurting, ribs most likely, the one most vulnerable. So why did she now feel cast adrift?

Her old buddy, the front guard of the two, raised his semiautomatic, using it like a teacher's pointer. "You there." He gestured for Stone to move away, then glanced at Vaughn. "You, no move."

As if she could. Her knees were locked together, her

stomach was a solid lump of congealed fear and her hands were fisted into useless rams of indecision.

If she attacked, it left Stone defenseless, not a word she'd normally associate with the guy. But if she did nothing, were they in any better a position?

Not likely.

With a prayer to whatever god watched out for fools and women who should know better, she raised her chin to the forward goon.

"Hey, Boris. Want to go a little one-on-one?"

Either her rapid-fire English was beyond his comprehension or he was stunned by the question. Stone was; she read it in the sudden stillness of his stance, the glance he shot her way. The one she ignored.

She straightened, rolling her neck like some prizefighter in the ring. Monica Chetworth had used the same move right before she stomped the stuffing out of Lori Mannington in sixth grade on the school grounds of St. Margaret's Academy. Vaughn had been removed from the school shortly thereafter.

"Come on, big guy. You afraid a deb can take you?"

"Vaughn," Stone growled. "Not a good idea."

She glanced at him. "That's your problem, Stone. Too controlling to let someone else take the lead."

"Yeah, when the lead can get them killed."

She shrugged and faced the front Russian, who hadn't moved much, except for his gaze darting back and forth between her and Stone. She hadn't pegged him as a quick thinker, which meant, if they were going to follow Blade while the trail was still fresh, she'd have to be the one to move things along.

A smart man would ignore her, shoot them both, or contain them in the now empty room. She was hoping Boris was more pissed than smart. A pissed man one could manipulate into doing something stupid.

Stepping forward with a swagger that was mostly bluff, she curled her fingers in a forward come-and-get-it motion. "That's it, sweet cheeks. Show me what you've got. Betcha a hundred rubles I can take you down in less than five." She glanced at the second guard. "You be the timer."

"Vaughn...."

The hulk moved, either intrigued or so sure of himself with backup that pride forced him into action.

She didn't care why he moved; she was simply relieved he had.

With a spate of guttural Russian, he handed his weapon off to his buddy, then stepped forward. She heard Stone suck in a breath.

"Don't you dare interfere, Stone."

"Of all the—"

"I'm about to teach Boris here some ballet."

With that she charged, on point and faster than expected, judging by her opponent's expression. A quick pivot, right leg extended, and she nailed him in the middle of his rock-hard gut.

Little damage done, but her body vibrated from the impact.

He grunted and lowered his head. She sidestepped his first lunge.

He was quick. But she had determination on her side. He turned, swinging at her, high then low, a scissor action bound to connect with flesh given enough time.

"So," she breathed through her mouth, dancing just out of his reach. "If you don't like ballet, how about gymnastics?"

A quick tuck and roll followed. She used her legs as a battering ram. Coming up quick and hard, heels forefront, dead center into the guy's jewels. Vassily would have recognized the move.

Boris dropped.

The second guy paused, torn by his comrade's agonized groans and the suddenness of the move.

Vaughn took advantage of his indecision. Twisting into a side curl, then flip, she was on her feet and in his face before he knew what hit him. A sharp thrust of the flat of her palm into his nose doubled him over. Two double-fisted blows to his exposed neck took him down.

She didn't wait for a status report, grabbing the weapons he let clatter to the floor.

Both men lay moaning in fetal positions on the concrete floor.

"Come on, guys, into the room. Crawl if you have to."

They didn't require much prompting, though whether it was the guns she held or the look on her face, she didn't know.

Once the goons were inside the cell, she grabbed the

cell door and slammed it shut. Only then did she turn to look at Stone, leaning against the far wall by one shoulder, his legs crossed at the ankle.

"Well done, Monroe." He clapped his hands, though there was nothing condescending in his tone. "Remind me not to piss you off."

"Too late." She handed him one of the rifles and took a second look at him, at the brackets of pain around his eyes, the shallowness of his breathing, the sheen of sweat, his pallor. She kept her concern from her voice, though, as she asked, "What now?"

"You tell me." He pressed both shoulders against the wall. "Your Russian is getting away."

"I'm not leaving you here alone."

"You will if it's a direct order."

"As if I'm going to start taking orders now." They stood toe to toe. The battle she'd just fought was nothing compared to the one she faced now. Alone, Stone was too vulnerable. But if he came along, he could slow them down.

"Don't fight me on this one, Vaughn," he whispered, raising one trembling hand to brush hair from her face.

Damn him.

She closed her eyes. "Not without you. Team members don't leave team members." Another pillow project.

She expected grief from him. What she got instead was a quick tug forward and a kiss to end all kisses. It tasted of anger and fear and regret.

She pulled back, wordless. Leave it to Stone to confound her even now.

"That's a yes, then," she whispered as her breath was in short supply.

"Lead. But be careful."

There was nothing more to say.

She took point, cradling the confiscated weapon in her arm. And he thought she couldn't take orders.

With no way to contact her team and direct them to him, they were on their own. She reached the door first and shoved it open, realizing too late that was not the best way to approach the unknown.

Fortunately, no one was on the other side. For once, luck smiled on her.

She stood in what looked like a gravel driveway, one leading away from the main house. The warm evening light blinded her momentarily. Here, the sounds of gunfire were louder but muffled, as if happening inside the compound instead of outside.

A quick glance around clued her in to the fact she wasn't alone. Nearby she heard Italians shouting orders. Ahead, a number of patrol cars were parked, their telltale blue lights flashing against the sky. A dozen official motorcycles were hunkered against a far rock wall.

"Lower level clear," someone barked in English.

Which meant the house was being systematically contained. If the lower level was clear, that meant the worst was probably not yet over, since most of the bad guys had been in the upstairs bedrooms when the assault started. But her goal wasn't some sleazeball terrorist.

Where was Blade? Had he that much of a lead on her? Where would he be headed once he made it this far?

A bird trill sneaked though the other sounds, at odds with the tension both inside her and around. She glanced in the direction of the sound and caught a flicker of movement out of the corner of her eye.

Blade was at the edge of the grove of cyprus trees, his dark clothing melding with the early evening shadows. As she watched, he paused, then darted toward the first vehicle near him, a Morris Minor.

Before she could alert any of the assault team he was in it, revving the engine even as she sprinted toward him, Stone close behind. Obviously adrenaline and risk healed a guy faster than TLC.

An Italian man in uniform screamed after them. Another materialized before her, waving his hands, shouting commands. She plowed right into him, stumbled, righted herself and kept running.

A cloud of gravel dust swirled around her as squealing tires announced she was too late to stop Blade.

"Damn and double damn." What now? She bent double, catching her wind, her hands on her knees.

What were her options? She glanced at Stone just as a burst of gunfire erupted.

Bullets screamed around them.

They both dove.

But it wasn't quick enough. Not for Vaughn.

She plastered herself against the gravel driveway, chunks of sharp rocks biting into her hands and cheeks. She waited for her head to clear.

"Vaughn, you hear me?" Stone demanded. "You hit?"

"Yeah, I hear you."

Didn't mean she was ready to get chatty.

She glanced at her right arm, sure it was a wall of flames, surprised to see only a thin trickle of blood oozing from a gash running just below her shoulder.

It didn't even rate a bandage, as if she had one.

"You hurt?" he asked again.

"Only my pride." She scrambled to her feet, using a tree to shelter her. One across from where Stone crouched. "You see anything?"

"No."

"Think we can go ahead?"

"If we keep low."

Now he told her. Not that crawling on her stomach would have avoided the last hail of bullets. But she wasn't about to tell him she'd taken a hit. Not now, at least.

"Let's go," she mumbled, scrambling to her knees.

Panting breath and boot-shod feet pounded the ground behind her. Another moment and there would be no choice. They'd both be held as suspects until someone could vouch for her. And Blade would escape.

With a cat leap from the stone wall to the lower parking lot below, she angled toward the nearest vehicle. Her teeth ached from slamming the soles of her sandals onto the packed ground. Three yards forward and she found what she wanted.

A police motorcycle with keys dangling in the

ignition. It flashed chrome and power beneath its sleek lines, small but nothing to laugh at. Just what the doctor ordered to catch a fleeing Blade.

She swung a leg across the leather seat, wrapped sweaty fingers around handle grips and scrambled to remember what a former boyfriend had taught her about kick-starting an unfamiliar bike.

Behind her, Stone cursed, then jumped on as a passenger.

"Sure hope you know what you're doing."

With a Hail Mary for lessons learned no matter what the situation, she sucked in a deep breath as she opened the throttle. The metal beast screamed out of the lot.

"Hang on," she shouted to Stone, ignoring the throb in her arm, the effort it took to hold the handle, everything except catching Blade.

Wind whipped her hair and face as she drove like an Italian racecar driver, only faster as the bike swerved and righted beneath her awkward handling. Even with Stone behind her she earned catcalls and whistles from Italian males sauntering along the road. Up ahead, when the curves permitted, she caught glimpses of the car Blade had commandeered.

They were gaining on him.

The lake road was clogged with holiday travelers as Blade's car zipped dangerously in and out of traffic, earning rude gestures from startled drivers and the blare of more than one car horn. If the Italians were like any other drivers, they'd be speed-dialing the nearest *polizia* station about the crazy woman flying like a witch on a metal broomstick, her hair swirling about her, her passenger no doubt green around the gills. If her luck held, they'd soon have company trailing their bike. But would it be soon enough?

Without warning, Blade's brake lights glowed red as he took a hard left, away from the lake. The small car careened up a narrow alleyway, clipping a parked car.

She hugged the road behind him.

They flew past a sign indicating they'd reached the small town of Cernobbio. In past visits, Vaughn had loved its picturesque four-hundred-year-old houses and narrow cobbled streets. But now that she was on a bike, the paved stones jarred her jaw and slammed her neck back and forth like a bobble head. Stone's head clipped hers a few times for good measure. She'd no doubt hear about her skills as a motorcyclist from him. If they lived.

Both vehicles climbed the rough road higher and higher into the old town. The street, with hulking buildings built side by side, grew narrow and dark. They reached the main piazza, one usually filled with strolling pedestrians and tourists, a logistics nightmare in a life-and-death race.

Then the Morris Minor disappeared, swallowed by a gap between buildings that should have squashed it.

Vaughn could only react and follow.

Stone cursed in three languages against her ear and gripped tighter.

Too late, she saw what she was up against. The bike slammed down a series of elongated steps, each drop pounding bone against bone. Civilians flattened themselves against stone buildings to avoid being hit. Oaths and curses followed their downward spiral.

If her jaw wasn't gripped shut to keep it from coming unhinged, she'd have joined them.

Ahead, she caught sight of a flash of metal. Blade. She hadn't lost him.

Then sunlight appeared. Open space.

The lake lay dead ahead.

A dark dot appeared high on the horizon, growing larger as the bike hopscotched along the road. Down. Down. Down.

The dot took shape. Bubble cockpit. Tail rudder. Whirring blade.

Helitourists sightseeing or—

The bike fishtailed. Vaughn screamed, whipping to the left as she scrambled to hold on to the narrow hand-grips, the engine revving beneath her.

For what seemed like an eternity, she hung suspended, more off the bike than on. Then it righted. She slammed forward. Once again on the seat. Not secure, but still there, Stone still with her.

The helicopter blocked the evening dusk before her, silhouetted between buildings, the backdrop of the lake and sky behind it.

The road Blade had chosen headed straight for it. No detours. Just a low stone wall at the far end. A cliff leading to water beyond it.

He'd have no choice but to stop.

The chopper hung suspended in midair, hovering like a beast of prey at the mouth of a tunnel.

But Blade didn't slow. Instead, he increased his speed.

She watched events unfold as if in slow motion.

The sound of his engine revving. Helicopter blades beating fast and furious while suspended. Waiting. Anticipating.

The flash of sunlight against the chrome of the car as it slammed into the wall and lifted off.

Upside down it twirled. Over and over on itself. A somersault of metal dark against the sky.

The copter shifted, rising on a current of air.

All was silent as Vaughn skidded her bike into an S and the engine died away.

Blade's car hung before her. Then dropped. Shot out of the sky in a downward spiral. Disappearing from view.

She could say nothing. Do nothing.

She was off the bike, running to the jagged, gaping wall. Stone grabbed her arm. Her bad one. A scream escaped her.

Then the explosion.

It was over.

Chapter 25

Vaughn reached over from the bed, picking up her phone on the fourth ring, catching the name on caller ID. Her arm twinged with the effort.

"This had better be good, Alex."

"Why?"

"I have a very hunky, very willing man warming my bed."

"Good, so Stone's there, too."

Vaughn caught her laugh. "How did you—"

"Give us some credit." She must have turned away from the phone as Vaughn heard her shouting, "You owe me fifty."

"Whom are you talking to?" Vaughn asked.

"Kelly. She thought you'd hold out a little longer."

"You guys bet I'd get together with Stone?"

"Nah. We knew that'd be a given. We all bet on the when. I won."

"Who are we?"

"Kelly, Mandy, myself and Jayleen."

"Jayleen knows?"

"Anyone who's been anywhere near you two, especially since Italy, would have to be deaf, dumb and blind not to know what's going on."

"So much for privacy in this group."

"Get used to it, girlfriend. We're spooks now. We don't have any secrets from each other."

Just like that, the laughter slid away.

Alex was wrong. They weren't operatives. At least not Vaughn. It'd been a week since Lake Como. One full day to settle details with the Italian authorities. One day to settle details with the CIA, whose agents were in the helicopter. Five back in D.C.

Poor Blade.

She hadn't wanted it to end as it had, even though they had yet to recover his body. He'd been a friend, a good one, once. And he'd left her a message, at the very end. A cryptic note attached to the codes discovered in his study safe: *None of them know the real us, eh, Vaughn? Au revoir, for now.*

How like him to think, even as commandos closed in on him, that they'd meet again.

She swallowed, focusing instead on what might have

happened if her team and the CIA hadn't hooked up to bring Blade down.

"You there, Vaughn?"

"Yeah, I'm still here."

After Italy, she'd returned to her D.C. town house only to have Stone showing up thirty minutes later. It had seemed so right to step into his arms. No words spoken. No need to.

The last four days had been about recovery. And exploration. And forgetting, in each other's arms, what neither spoke about. Blade gone. Vaughn's new career in limbo. A lot more left unspoken than spoken.

"Good, you listening?" Alex continued. "Ling Mai wants to see you ASAP. And Stone, too."

Why? She understood the Stone part; he was still a member of the team. But why would Ling Mai want to see her? To drop the final ax?

The mission had been declared a success. Not that the acknowledgement mattered. But while Ling Mai had offered congratulations, she had also chopped Vaughn off at the knees. Director Werner had made it clear. While the Agency and its new team of Invisible Recruits had proven their worth, one member had been requested to leave the team or suffer the consequences.

Ling Mai hadn't translated Vaughn's father's words verbatim, but Vaughn had got the drift. If Vaughn stayed, the Agency could forfeit any future assignments working for or with the CIA.

Vaughn understood only too well how power and politics worked. Ling Mai did not need to pretty it up for her. Ling Mai had used phrases such as *much-needed rest* and *time away* for a period. Vaughn hadn't waited around to hear the details.

So here she was, working at getting her thoughts around the hole in her world. What now? Back to her old life? Not likely, but no other options came to mind. Charity work, maybe. Wasn't that what women from her social circle did to feel useful? No dirty hands or broken nails, but more fetes and receptions and arranging dinners and auctions.

Vaughn was going to be physically ill.

"Tell her we'll be there in an hour." Vaughn slowly hung up the phone, turning to see Stone leaning against the bedroom doorjamb.

Damn, he was one sexy man. Rumpled by what sleep they'd managed to get. Stubble darkening the angle of his rock-hewn jaw. His eyes hooded and enigmatic.

"Ling Mai?"

"Yeah." Vaughn shrugged, willing some flexibility into her tensed neck and back. The good news was her stomach was calm. Maybe she was getting the hang of this lifestyle. Right before it disappeared forever.

Stone remained quiet on the drive to Maryland. Not that she blamed him. What was there to say? It's been nice? See you at the grocery store sometime? People who made the choices they made didn't have lives. Not real ones.

Stone had learned that a long time ago.

But she was a quick study.

It wasn't until they walked up the rock steps to the

main house that his shoulder brushed hers. A clumsy move for a man like Stone, one that had her stopping.

"She won't eat you." His gaze scanned hers.

"Easy for you to say."

Stone moved as if he were going to speak, but another voice interrupted.

"There you are," Alex hailed, exiting from a Jeep Wrangler, with Kelly, Mandy and Jayleen hot on her heels.

Vaughn closed her eyes. She so didn't want this. Getting the final boot was bad enough. In front of the women she'd come to think of as friends, as partners, was so much worse.

"Come on, Vaughn, it's only been a few days. Okay, a week, but you're not going to shut us out that easily."

Alex and Kelly walked up beside her. Jayleen and Mandy hung back. Wise women, those two, who either sensed where Vaughn was at or had enough instincts to walk warily around a wounded beast.

"Go away." There, she'd said it openly, no longer sugarcoated.

"No can do." Kelly sounded so chipper, you'd have thought she was some camp counselor cheering on her young charges. "We worked too hard to track you down." The blonde turned to Jayleen. "You owe me a twenty. I was right."

Against her better judgment, Vaughn asked, "Right about what?"

"Right about you moping," Jayleen shot back.

"I'm not moping."

"Sure looks like it to me." The black woman glanced

toward Stone. "Poor little rich girl got her feelings bent out of shape so she gets to be a victim."

Oh, that was priceless. Vaughn clenched her jaw, anger and hurt bubbling soul-deep. "You don't have a bloody clue what you're talking about."

"Ladies." Kelly stepped between the two women, always the peacemaker. "What I think Jayleen's trying to say is we were worried about you."

Fat chance. Vaughn glared at Jayleen, who glared right back, then grinned, taking the wind right out of Vaughn's sails.

"Go away, guys. I'm late for meeting Ling Mai."

"Then we'll be here when you're done." Alex glanced at the others, then back at Vaughn. "And do not sneak out the back door. We have super-secret techno things to find you with."

"Yeah," Jayleen drawled. "And sometimes they work."

Lord, she was going to miss these women. And if she didn't leave now, she'd turn into a blubbering mess.

"You ready?" Stone asked.

She nodded and followed him inside, careening into his back when he stopped again before he was supposed to.

"What?" she asked, glancing at the empty foyer.

"You're not alone, princess."

Great, just when she thought she had a handle on her emotions, he had to go and yank the rug out from under her.

But Ling Mai was waiting. First things first.

"Good." She rolled her neck, trying for a casual

tone. "I'll remember two heads can get chopped off as easily as one."

"Another pillow to embroider?"

He remembered. She couldn't help the smile. Especially as his actually reached his eyes.

So this whole fiasco hadn't been a complete waste. Some good had come of it.

A security guard stepped from behind the director's door. "Agent Stone, Ling Mai would like you to wait in the green room."

Stone gave her a salute before he headed down the hallway.

Vaughn used her debutante training as she followed the guard. Shoulders straight, head up, smile in place. She might be going down in a hail of misery, but she'd go in true deb style.

The guard nodded to Ling Mai's private office.

Vaughn tightened her smile. Another nanosecond and it would crack. She stepped inside the office.

"Vaughn."

Ling Mai was her normal regal self behind her desk. Calm. Poised. Looking as serene as the Chinese goddess Kuan Yin.

Vaughn inhaled deeply. The best defense was a good offense. Another pillow cover. "For the record," she said, "Stone and the others acted on my directions. Any irregularities in procedure are my sole responsibility."

"Is that so?"

How could three words sound so bland?

"Yes."

"Then you are not giving your fellow agents much credit." Ling Mai stood, walked around the desk and motioned for Vaughn to sit. "Nor yourself."

What was she saying? And why couldn't she say it straight out?

"Before you and I talk, there is someone else here to see you."

Since only one person knew she was here, only one person could be waiting. Her father. Vaughn bit back a groan, but Ling Mai was watching her closely.

"I'm sorry," Vaughn offered.

"For?"

"For bringing my personal life into the Agency. For causing you and the team problems."

"That is what we deal with every day, Vaughn. Problems. It is our specialty."

"But he has no right to threaten you."

"Do I appear threatened?"

"No. But then you never do."

Ling Mai laughed. "We shall talk later. But before I leave, let me assure you that, if you had let me continue the other day, I could have reassured you that I do not take kindly to blackmail."

She left before Vaughn could find any words.

Her father entered the room, no less forceful than before. But something was different. What, she couldn't put her finger on, but something.

She waited, refusing to rise from the chair though the need to pace was great.

"Father."

"Vaughn."

Well, that was pleasant.

Her father crossed to the desk but remained standing. He cleared his throat before speaking. "They have not yet found Golumokoff's body. The lake is particularly deep there."

"Have they located his car?"

"Yes. And the control was in it. But no sign yet of Golumokoff."

She had been there. No way could anyone have survived that crash. No way.

She said nothing. There was nothing to say. He had saved her life once. And, when the opportunity came, twice; to eliminate her and Stone, he'd let them live. Then there was the fact that several wanted terrorists were rounded up at Blade's home. He may not have intended that to happen, but it did anyway. She'd like to think some good had come out of so much ugliness.

"Vaughn." Her father cleared his throat and looked uncomfortable. A first for him. "I've had a long conversation with Ling Mai."

"Yes?"

"As diplomatic a woman as she is, she can also be very clear in setting the record straight."

"About?"

"About when an old man oversteps his authority and crosses the line separating director of operations and father."

When she said nothing, he continued, "I was

wrong. It was with the best of intentions, but I was wrong and I endangered not only you and Stone, but your operation. Which is unforgivable for a man in my position."

This time, she did stand. Too much bubbled and churned within her not to.

"What exactly are you saying, Father?"

"It means that you are good at what you're choosing to do. It would not be my choice for you. And every day I will continue to worry and fear, and Lord knows how I'm going to explain things to your mother, but it is still your life—not mine—to direct. Not any more. My job is done."

It was not emotion blurring her vision. Operatives did not go all warm and fuzzy at the drop of a hat. She was sure Stone had taught her that. On day one, no doubt.

"So there will be no reprisals against Ling Mai and the Agency?" Her voice quivered, but only a little.

He barked a short, rough laugh. "Ling Mai was gracious enough to explain to me that I need her more than she needs me."

"And Stone? There will be no reprisals against him?"

"Only if he hurts you." Her father's voice deepened. "And then there's no place on this earth he can hide."

She stepped forward, no longer ashamed of the tear slipping from the corner of her eye. "Thank you."

She hugged her father. He embraced her, his arms stiff and awkward around her, but there.

"About Mother," she said, when she had stepped back, wiping tears from her eyes. "We could always lie."

"And wait for her to find out?" Her father shook

his head. "Easier for you, my dear. I must live with the woman."

"Then I'll tell her." She raised a hand before he could interrupt. "In my own way. My own time."

"But in this century?"

She grinned. "If I must. Yes, in this century."

He brushed a strand of hair back from her damp cheek. "You go safely."

"Of course. Always."

He snorted. A very undignified, undiplomatic snort. "Ling Mai told me you were very much like myself. I guess I was afraid to look too closely to see the truth. But she was right."

"Take care, Father." Her smile felt real this time, and long overdue.

"Of course. Always." He closed the door gently behind him.

Vaughn stood there, engulfed by the silence, not quite sure if she should hunt Ling Mai down and say...what? False alarm? The Agency would be safe from reprisal? Could she come back and be part of the team?

But before she could formulate a plan, the door shot open and Stone stood there.

"Good. Let's go."

She followed, asking, "Where?"

"Qatar. Hostage situation in a very exclusive expatriate housing development."

"Tariq in Doha?" she asked, following closely as he headed down the hallway.

He paused. "Don't tell me. Another boyfriend?"

"His sister. Qatar is the world's richest oil-producing country. A lot of people enjoy its amenities."

"Only people you know, princess."

"That a problem?"

"Not anymore." He grinned.

"But what about Ling Mai?" she asked.

"What about her?"

"Don't be dense, Stone. I don't know if I'm an agent or not."

He laughed outright. "Of course you're an agent. You never weren't one."

"But—"

"We've got to get moving here, princess. You in or out?"

"In." It came on a whoosh of breath and felt right.

So very, very right.

They were almost to the command center when she stopped him again.

"What now?"

"You never told me what M.T. stands for." If she didn't find out right then and there, she never would. That was the problem with dealing with spooks. They were cagey. This one more than most.

He looked as if he wanted to refuse. Or shake her. But then she was used to that look.

"What is it, Stone? Malcolm Tennsion? Mark Taylor? What?"

"Monday, Tuesday."

"What?"

"You heard me."

"You were named for days of the week?"

"Yeah." He actually looked sheepish, glancing around to make sure they were still alone. "My mother always said it took her two days to give birth to me and I was never to forget it."

She would not laugh. No matter how tempting. Not if she wanted to live to see a new day.

Instead, she stood on her tiptoes and brushed a kiss across his stubble-darkened cheek. "That's so sweet."

"You tell anyone, princess, and—"

"And?" This time she did grin.

"Don't push it."

"Never."

"Like I believe that. Get inside, deb." He pointed to the door. "A mission awaits."

A mission and a life.

It didn't get any better than this.

*Can't get enough Silhouette Bombshell?
Every month we've got four unique
and entertaining reads
featuring strong, sexy, savvy women
and the men who challenge them.
Don't miss a single thrilling moment!*

*Turn the page for an exclusive preview
of one of next month's releases,*

*THE FIREBIRD DECEPTION
by Cate Dermody*

Available June 2006 at your favorite retail outlet.

A shadow separated itself from the darkness, black against the shaded grays and browns of a mountaintop night. Human in size, male in form, moving quickly and silently over stone and rubble. A dip in the craggy rock highlighted his profile against rich midnight blue sky, the faint colors of stars glittering as if caught in his hair.

Alisha went absolutely still, muscles in her arms trembling with the strain of holding herself from a ledge, fingertips dug into the stone. As long as she remained motionless, she would be no more than he had been, one undiscovered shadow amongst thousands. She could see the path he took from the corner of her eye, could watch him enter farther into her line of vision. In a moment he crossed out of it, blocked from sight by her own aching biceps. Alisha curled her upper lip and cautiously lowered herself until her feet touched the earth, her weight barely disturbing the loose stone. She remained where she was a few seconds, forehead pressed against her still-uplifted arm while she tried to find a curse that was worth mouthing in the silence of the Pyrenees night.

It would be easy to forget who she was in the silence of the mountain night. Easy to become nothing more than what she appeared—a young woman hiking and climbing alone. An adventurer, or a woman so intent on earning solitude that safety was a secondary concern.

It would be easy to forget, at least, if there was not another climber on the mountain, moving as quietly and quickly as Alisha herself. He had no more business there than she did, which meant it was extremely unlikely that his business was the same as her own.

Somewhere not far ahead of her lay the black box from a downed American military spycraft, injured by a hand-carried earth-to-sky missile and wrecked in the Spanish mountains. The CIA was not supposed to be spying on its allies, and outside discovery of the craft's remains would cause a furor at best. At worst it would reopen the breach between so-called Old Europe and the United States. All she had to do was retrieve the black box. Any other remains were expected to be cremated by the crash as to be unidentifiable.

It was supposed to be a routine mission, Alisha thought wryly. No complications. Get in, get the goods, get out.

What was supposed to be almost never was.

Alisha pushed away from the rock face, turning her attention to the shale and granite beneath her feet. This high up, there was comparatively little loose stone, which was good: it would allow her to approach her competitor with almost no warning.

She ran on her toes, gaze flickering from the ground in front of her to the shadows ahead of her, watching for the man's movements in the darkness. A pack hugged her back, what gear she required huddled there, muffled so metal couldn't clang and echo against the mountainsides, announcing her presence to whomever might be listening.

And someone was. Alisha hesitated at a sharp bend in the stone, calming her breathing before she cautiously glanced around the edge of rock. A runoff channel, left by millennia of melting snow water, bent around a switchback. It was the easiest course to take since her goal lay just beyond the switchback, only a little higher up on the mountainside. Had she been there first, it was the track she'd have taken. She could see the shape of her rival's body farther up that trail, and slipped behind the outcropping again, examining her other options.

The cliff that the switchback snaked around wasn't quite sheer. Alisha studied it from her vantage point in the shadows, then slipped her backpack off. Even when she'd had all night and no competition, climbing with only the faint light of the crescent moon and her own judgment had been a challenge. With someone already ahead of her, it was wiser, if less thrilling, to rely on the technology she had at hand. She grabbed her night goggles, which fit snugly over her face, weighing little more than sunglasses.

The world went vividly green. Alisha took a few seconds, waiting until she was confident of the oddly colored brights and darknesses. She shrugged her backpack on again, fastening it around her waist with a knot instead of the plastic clip meant to hold it. Alisha grinned a little and stretched tall to work her fingers over a ledge hardly deeper than her first knuckle.

It was enough to give her purchase, enough to allow her a slow bicep burn as she drew herself higher with upper-body strength alone. She liked to think of it as her gift, her secret weapon, a physical capability beyond most women. One which she had few opportunities to show off. The whole point of a secret weapon was to only use it when necessary.

Gravel slipped under her fingers, sending her jolting down several inches before her feet caught the last ledge she'd stood on. She leaned into the cool rock face, trying to breathe steadily instead of taking gulps of air past the knot of panic in her throat.

"Look up," she whispered to herself, silently. Focusing on the fall was a sure way to work herself into making it. Alisha turned her gaze upward again, examining the crevasses and juts of the stone. *Nearly to the top,* she promised herself. And then she'd see what there was to be seen.

She drew herself over the ravine's edge, muscles relaxing in a moment's relief for the change of position.

She was alone. The switchback trail must have been longer than she'd guessed it to be: the man hadn't yet reappeared.

Footsteps, almost noiseless against the rock, sounded behind her. Alisha faded farther into the shadows, hidden behind the boulder. Peering out afforded her a view of most of the canyon. It was only moments before the man appeared, dark-haired and broad-shouldered in the green vision of Alisha's night goggles. He hesitated just beyond the boulder, studying the ravine just as Alisha had done. She drew in her next breath slowly, deliberately, as if doing so might turn her invisible to his gaze and ears.

Instead, he turned toward her more fully, still examining the canyon, as if she'd betrayed herself with that breath.

And she did, as his profile came into focus, pale against the dark green sky and mountains. Good sense and training were thrown away in a wash of anger and disbelief. Alisha stood, yanking the night goggles off and throwing them to the side in pure outrage.

"Reichart."

**HOTEL
MARCHAND**

**Four sisters.
A family legacy.
And someone is out to destroy it.**

A captivating new limited continuity, launching June 2006

The most beautiful hotel in New Orleans,
and someone is out to destroy it. But mystery,
danger and some surprising family revelations
and discoveries won't stop the Marchand sisters
from protecting their birthright…
and finding love along the way.

SPECIAL PRICE!

This riveting new saga begins with

In the Dark

by national bestselling author

JUDITH ARNOLD

The party at Hotel Marchand is in full swing when the lights suddenly go out. What does head of security Mac Jensen do first? He's torn between two jobs—protecting the guests at the hotel and keeping the woman he loves safe.

A woman to protect. A hotel to secure. And no idea who's determined to harm them.

On Sale June 2006

HMITD

**Hidden in the secrets of antiquity,
lies the unimagined truth...**

Introducing

a brand-new line filled with mystery
and suspense, action and adventure,
and a fascinating look into history.

And it all begins with DESTINY.

In a sealed crypt in
France, where the
terrifying legend of
the beast of Gevaudan
begins to unravel,
Annja Creed discovers
a stunning artifact
that will seal her destiny.

*Available every other
month starting
July 2006, wherever
you buy books.*

GRA1

Page-turning drama...

Exotic, glamorous locations...

Intense emotion and passionate seduction...

Sheikhs, princes and billionaire tycoons...

This summer, may we suggest:

THE SHEIKH'S
DISOBEDIENT BRIDE
by Jane Porter
On sale June.

AT THE GREEK TYCOON'S
BIDDING
by Cathy Williams
On sale July.

THE ITALIAN MILLIONAIRE'S
VIRGIN WIFE
On sale August.

With new titles to choose from every month,
discover a world of romance in our books written
by internationally bestselling authors.